## ACCLAIM FOR THE NOVEL

"Opal Carew is a genius at spinning the m... ...... ......, .......
into forbidden fantasies and visiting emotions that literally bring the
characters to their knees. A steamy-hot read!"

—*Fresh Fiction* on *Pleasure Bound*

"Carew's book reminds me of a really good box of chocolates that you
want to savor, but can't help eating all up in one sitting because it's so
decadent and yummy. Feast on this one today!"

—*Night Owl Romance* on *Bliss*

"This romance is emotional, highly erotic, and most definitely a
guaranteed keeper—in other words, it was written by Opal Carew!"

—*Reader to Reader* on *Bliss*

"A blazing-hot erotic romp...a must-read for lovers of erotic romance. A
fabulously fun and stupendously steamy read for a cold winter's
night. This one's so hot, you might need to wear oven mitts while
you're reading it!"

—*Romance Junkies*

"Fresh, exciting, and extremely sexual, with characters you'll fall in
love with. Absolutely fantastic!"

—*Fresh Fiction*

"Carew pulls off another scorcher....She knows how to write a love
scene that takes her reader to dizzying heights of pleasure."

—*My Romance Story*

"Opal Carew brings erotic romance to a whole new level....She writes a
compelling romance and sets your senses on fire with her love
scenes!"

—*Reader to Reader*

ALSO BY OPAL CAREW

# Insatiable

## Opal Carew

St. Martin's Griffin

New York

INSATIABLE. Copyright © 2012 by Opal Carew. All rights reserved. Printed in the United States of America. For information, address St. Martin's Press, 175 Fifth Avenue, New York, N.Y. 10010.

www.stmartins.com

Library of Congress Cataloging-in-Publication Data

Carew, Opal.
    Insatiable : a novel / Opal Carew—1st ed.
       p.   cm.
    ISBN 978-0-312-67461-8 (pbk.)
    ISBN 978-1-4299-3849-5 (e-book)
  I.  Title.
    PR9199.4.C367I57   2012
    813'.6—dc23
                  2011035996

10 9 8 7 6 5 4 3

Dedicated to Star.

I miss you.

# Acknowledgments

As always, my heartfelt thanks to Rose, Emily, Colette, Mark, Matt, and Jason.

# Insatiable

# One

Evan watched Crystal walk down the stairs in her satin gown, her face glowing, and his heart compressed. God, but he loved her. His hands shook at the thought she'd be uttering her wedding vows in front of a minister and a huge congregation of family and friends in a very short time.

Too short a time.

He'd spent all last night thinking about it. Realizing this was his last chance. If he didn't do something now, then the events that had been so long in the planning would proceed, and the future would be set.

And he would be miserable.

He had to talk to her. He had to tell her how he felt. Explain why he hadn't told her sooner. Why he was ruining her wedding day. And probably ruining their relationship forever.

But he had to do something. Because in less than an hour she would marry another man—Evan's best friend.

And Evan couldn't let that happen without speaking up and telling her how much he loved her. Because maybe . . . just maybe . . . she felt the same way about him.

No matter what Evan did, his friendship with Brent was probably over. And certainly, if Crystal turned Evan down . . . *oh, God, please don't let her turn me down* . . . things would always be strained between them. But he had to know. He could not spend the rest of his life regretting not telling her. Not at least reaching out for the happiness he so desired. Being with the only woman he had ever loved.

She laughed at something her older sister, Renee, said to her, then they both disappeared into the study. The wedding was taking place at her family home, a big old sprawling house on the lake, with a couple of acres surrounding it. The groom wouldn't arrive for another thirty minutes, so Evan knew he had to make his move now.

Damn it, he wished he'd talked to her sooner. He'd had months to speak up, but he hadn't wanted to do anything to hurt his friendship with Brent or to potentially hurt Crystal's happiness. But as the wedding had drawn nearer, he'd realized that his happiness was every bit as important as Brent's. And Crystal deserved to know how Evan felt about her. She might turn him down, but at least she would be offered the choice. If she chose Brent, Evan would understand, no matter how much it shattered his chance at happiness. He would respect her choice. But he had to at least offer that choice.

His hands shook and he curled them into fists. Renee left the study and Evan took a step forward. For a split second, thoughts of abandoning this insane idea flashed through his brain, but he quelled them and took another step, then another, until he was almost at the door.

"Hey, Evan. You look absolutely dashing in that tux."

His gaze shot to Renee, who walked toward the door with a glass of water in her hand.

"Uh . . . are you taking that in to Crystal?" he asked, feeling like an idiot asking the obvious.

She grinned. "Yeah. You know, you look as nervous as the groom probably does."

"It's a big day," he said, repeating what he'd heard echoed around him all morning.

He'd been here for two hours helping to set up and hoping to get a chance to talk to Crystal, but she'd been off to the hairdresser, then holed up in her room getting ready. He had never intended to leave it to the final moments to talk to her.

"Do you mind if I take it in?" he asked. "I wanted to talk to her before things begin."

"Want to wish her luck?" She handed him the glass. "Sure, go ahead. I'll go find the bouquets and distribute the boutonnieres to the guys."

"Great. Thanks."

Renee turned and headed toward the big country kitchen at the front of the house.

Evan sucked in a deep breath, then knocked on the door.

Crystal stared out the sliding doors that led to the large wooden deck overlooking the lake outside. She'd grown up in this house, enjoyed the pleasures of living in a big rambling home with lots of room to play with her friends and her three siblings, all older than her.

Sunlight glittered on the rippling water. It was a beautiful day for a wedding.

Her wedding. She could hardly believe it.

Soon she and Brent would be husband and wife. She smiled at the thought of walking down the makeshift aisle, among all her friends and family, and joining with the man she loved. And she had loved Brent for a long time. She couldn't believe this day was finally here.

Her stomach quivered, and she patted it. Nerves. Not due to second thoughts about the life-altering events of today. She just worried that something might go wrong. Of course, that was every bride's fear, but it kept niggling at her no matter how much she tried to brush it aside.

A knock sounded at the door. Renee would be returning with water, but she wouldn't knock. Could it be Brent? As much as she'd love to see his smiling face, it was bad luck for the groom to see the bride before the wedding. That's why she'd asked her mother's friend and neighbor, Georgia, if Brent and his sister, Lily, could stay at her house last night.

"Yes?" she asked, not willing to risk answering the door.

"Crystal, it's Evan. May I come in?"

She smiled. Evan. He was Brent's best friend, and over the past two years, she had gotten to know him well. He was a real sweetheart. And sexy as all get-out, but she felt guilty for even noticing that.

*Geez, I'm not dead. There's nothing wrong with noticing. It's doing something about it that's wrong.*

The door opened and Evan peered into the room. He slipped inside and closed the door behind him.

God, he was gorgeous. And every time she got near him, her insides quivered. She patted her stomach again.

*It's okay to notice. It really is okay to notice.* That had almost become a mantra for her. So she felt an attraction to Evan? She *loved* Brent. And that wouldn't change, no matter how many men made her heart go pitter-pat.

She'd just thought that once she found her true love, the pitter-pat thing wouldn't happen anymore. But this was the real world, not storybook land. The reality was that an attractive man could make her take notice.

But she loved Brent.

"I brought you this." Evan handed her a glass of water. "Renee was bringing it to you."

"Thanks." She took the glass from his hand, ignoring the ripple of awareness that quivered through her when their fingers touched.

*It's okay to notice.*

Evan's stomach twisted, but he had no time to let nerves slow him down. If he started thinking about how close he and Brent were, how much damage this would do to their deep friendship, then he knew he'd back down. But he had to do this. For the *good* of their relationship. If this went unspoken between him and Crystal, it would eat away at him and their friendship until it all fell apart.

"I . . . uh . . . wanted to talk to you, if you've got a few minutes. I mean, I know the wedding starts soon, but—"

Another knock sounded at the door.

"Yes?" Crystal said.

Renee popped her head in the door. "Crystal, Mom wants to go over some details with you again, and Dad's anxious to use the den. I think he wants a quick drink before the ceremony. He's nervous . . . it's so cute. I think I can hold Mom off—they're things you've been over a dozen times already—but I suggest you make yourself scarce or you'll keep being interrupted." She smiled brightly. "Maybe take a walk. That'll keep you calm and relaxed."

"In my dress?"

Renee came into the room with a robe draped over her arm and dangled a pair of sandals in front of her. "I would think you'd be more concerned about those high heels, so I brought you these, and a robe." She closed the door behind her.

"I'll walk with you, if that's all right," Evan said.

He would be more comfortable—or rather, less uncomfortable—talking to her about this somewhere other than her family home.

"That's a great idea. You can run interference." Renee turned and winked at him, as though they shared a secret.

Damn, did she know? He'd met Renee once in San Diego, when she'd come to visit Crystal, then he'd spent a little time with her over the past week while he and

Brent had been staying in her hometown of Emerald Haven, Oregon. Had she somehow figured out his feelings for Crystal?

"I wouldn't mind getting some fresh air," Crystal said, "but Evan has to be here when Brent arrives and—"

Renee waved away her words. "That's almost half an hour from now. Don't worry about it. Just go for your walk."

Crystal glanced at Evan, but Renee just smiled. "Evan, turn around, okay?"

Evan felt his face drain of color as he realized Crystal was going to strip off her wedding gown right here in the same room as him. He turned around as instructed. The sound of her zipper gliding down, then the rustle of fabric, made his breath come quicker.

"Okay, done," Renee said. "You can turn around again."

Evan turned to see Crystal now wearing a long white satin robe and sandals.


Crystal watched Renee hang her gown on the satin hanger she'd brought with her, then turned to Evan. "Okay, let's go."

She followed him to the sliding doors in the den that led to the deck so they could slip away without being pulled into last minute preparations. As she stepped outside, the soft breeze brushed across her cheek and she breathed in the fresh air. The house was filled with the aroma of bacon left over from the big breakfast Mom had prepared for everyone this morning, so it felt good to clear her lungs.

"Renee's right. If Mom sees me, she'll start asking all kinds of questions, because that's what Mom does. She wants everything to be perfect, so she fusses over every detail." She lifted the skirt of her robe as she walked along the wooden deck.

Evan took her hand as she approached the stairway, which she appreciated as she negotiated the six steps while lifting the long robe so she wouldn't trip. The robe was actually Renee's, so it was a little big on her. Finally she reached the bottom, then stepped onto the granite patio. Her dad had built the patio himself, with the help of her and her brother Tim. Not that they'd been that much help, at only seven and ten, but they'd tried, and Dad had seemed to love having them underfoot.

As they walked across the lawn toward the water, she realized Evan hadn't let go of her hand yet. And it felt nice enveloped in his.

Too nice.

She tried to draw it away, then stumbled on the robe. He tightened his hold as he steadied her. He was leading her to her favorite place. Nestled in the trees, over-looking the water, it was a perfect place to find solitude and think things over. She'd shown it to Brent and Evan this week while taking them around her childhood haunts.

But going there now with Evan . . . alone . . .

Her stomach fluttered again. Nerves for sure, but something more bothered her. Because her insides hinted that she'd love to do more than talk to Evan right now.

As they stepped through the opening between the trees, the thought shocked her.

She loved Brent. Why did her body always react this way to Evan? And why would her thoughts turn to how exciting it would be to feel his full lips on hers? To be held in his arms?

At first, she'd been sure it was just because she feared the same thing happening that had happened when she'd first met Brent. It had been in college when she'd been engaged to someone from back home. She'd felt guilty about the attraction she'd felt for Brent, even though she'd never acted on it. Right after graduation, she and Gary got married, but the marriage didn't last very long. She came to realize that her feelings for Gary had been more a desire to keep a connection with home than they were for the man. And Gary must have felt the same, because he'd been more than happy to throw in the towel on their marriage. She'd moved to San Diego to start a new life. Crystal had looked Brent up right after the divorce finalized and discovered that what she'd always felt for Brent had been real desire. And that had turned to real love.

So when she'd met Evan, Brent's best friend, and felt the same racing heart and heated attraction, she'd ignored it, assuming a part of her was trying to sabotage her relationship with Brent because she was afraid she'd fail again.

She knew she loved Brent, so there was no reason for her to fall for another guy.

Especially his best friend.

They reached the small gazebo near the edge of the water that her father had built when he'd realized how much she liked this place. Evan helped her up the single step. The water rippled along the shore, and a loon's lonely cry echoed across the water.

Then Evan took both her hands and gazed into her eyes. The heat in those forest green eyes sent her stomach into somersaults.

He cleared his throat. "Crystal, I have something I need to tell you."

# Two

Brent sat on the deck enjoying the warm sunshine as he stared at the glittering surface of the lake. He was staying with Georgia, a friend of Crystal's mother. Her house was just a few lots down the shore from Crystal's parents' house. Georgia had gone over to Crystal's house a couple of hours ago to help with preparations.

He sipped his coffee as he stretched his tuxedo-clad legs in front of him, thoughts of Crystal's beautiful face swirling through his mind and how in less than an hour she would become his wife. Then tomorrow, they would fly off to the Cayman Islands and a sumptuous honeymoon in a luxurious villa, a great trip Crystal had actually won in a sweepstakes six months ago. Perfect timing for their honeymoon. In fact, it was what had prompted him to pop the question when he did.

He had waited so long to finally get the chance to date her, even though they'd felt the powerful chemistry between them for years.

He'd met her back in college, but she'd been engaged to another guy. The attraction between Brent and Crystal had been instant and overwhelming, but there was no way either of them would act on it, given the situation.

Before meeting Crystal, he'd never believed in love at first sight, but even after he'd graduated and moved to San Diego, he'd never stopped thinking about her. The day she'd called him up to tell him she was single again and living in San Diego, too, he'd been thrilled. As soon as they saw each other again, the sizzling heat between them flared.

She had been as eager to explore the intense attraction between them as he had. That was the day true happiness had entered his life. He shifted on the deck chair. But hand in hand with grasping a dream came the fear of losing it.

For some reason, deep in his gut, he worried that he would lose her. An insecurity he hated falling prey to.

A part of him wanted to rush over to her house and talk to her. Assure himself that this dream come true was not about to be shattered.

He placed his cup on the wooden table beside the chair and stood up, then walked to the end of the deck. He gazed in the direction of Crystal's parents' house. He couldn't see it through the trees, but he knew there'd be lots of people rushing around, putting final touches on the decorations and flowers. People would be arriving soon, then the ushers would show them to their chairs, laid out in neat rows on the huge lawn beside the water.

He and Crystal had driven to Emerald Haven a week

before the wedding so he could meet her family and they could all get to know one another. Crystal had taken him on a tour of the beautiful lakefront property her parents owned, and she'd shown him her favorite place, where she liked to go to think and to calm her mind.

He paced across the deck. It was the waiting that was driving him crazy. His sister, Lily, was still in the shower, and she'd need about twenty minutes after that to get ready. Until then he was alone with his thoughts. Brent sighed. Being with Crystal would calm him. But since he couldn't see her before the wedding, maybe he'd head over to the lovely secluded place she liked to go. Her private place. There he'd be able to feel her presence.

He smiled and walked down the steps, then along the dirt path. It wasn't very far, only a few hundred yards. As he walked, he thought he saw a flash of white through the trees.

As Crystal gazed into Evan's deep green eyes, panic lurched through her. The heat in his eyes . . . the intensity of his gaze . . . Oh, God, whatever he was going to say, she was sure she didn't want to hear it.

She backed away a little.

"You know, Evan, the wedding is in just a few minutes and I really should get back. Let's talk later."

As she tried to turn away, to make her escape, he grasped her arms gently.

"But that will be too late." Urgency filled his words. "What I need to tell you must be said now."

He drew her back to face him, and her protest died in her throat as she became mesmerized by the intense emotion in his eyes.

She knew what he was going to say. God help her, once the words were out, nothing could be the same again. If she could only stop him. Leave things the way they were between them. As long as he didn't say the words . . . but her throat clenched so tight, she couldn't make a protest.

"Crystal, I'm in love with you."

Evan watched her eyes shimmer, as if about to shed tears. His chest compressed painfully. All his hopes shattered in that moment.

But he wasn't ready to give up. He'd come this far.

"Why are you telling me this?" Her voice trembled.

"I'm sorry, Crystal. I know this isn't fair. I'd never meant to tell you, but I realized that you deserve to know. You deserve the opportunity to make a choice. If you choose Brent—"

"I already did."

"I know, but you didn't know I love you, too. If you still choose Brent, I'll understand. But at least I'll have taken a chance on happiness. If I never said anything . . . if you never knew how I felt about you . . ." He squeezed her arm gently. "I'm sorry, Crystal, but I was gambling on a lifetime of happiness and I couldn't let that just slip away. Not without finding out how you feel."

14

---

The pain in his green eyes tore at Crystal's heart.

"Oh, God, Evan. I'm so sorry." She reached out and stroked his cheek. "I don't want to hurt you."

The second her fingers brushed against his skin, she knew she was lost. Emotions buried deep inside spiraled through her and erupted in a painful swirling confusion.

His hand slid around her back and he drew her forward. His face lowered to hers and the moment their lips brushed, she was spellbound. His mouth moved on hers, gently at first, in a sweet, blissful caress, then his tongue slipped inside and seduced her with a sweet, passionate, tumultuous kiss.

Her heart rate accelerated, and she melted against him. Her arms wrapped around him, and the feel of his big, muscular body against hers, his arms around her making her feel soft and protected, sent her hormones into a spin.

There was a reason she shouldn't be doing this. A very important reason. But right now, she couldn't think what it was.

His tongue swirled inside her and her tongue coiled around his. They undulated together. She stroked his smooth, freshly shaven cheek and breathed in his musky aftershave. A need built within her. For this man. Not sexual. Something deep and indefinable. She wanted to be with him. To have him be a part of her life forever.

With a start, she drew away.

But what about Brent?

———

Evan's heart soared. A woman didn't kiss a man like that if she didn't have feelings for him. He could feel sweet love in her touch. In the way her lips caressed his. In the delicate touch of her hand on his cheek.

But when her lips drew away, she stared at him with panic in her eyes.

Then they shimmered . . . and tears swelled.

"Crystal?"

"I . . ."

She gulped in a breath, but before she could speak, he rushed ahead, intent on preventing her from uttering the words he knew would come.

"Crystal, you obviously share my feelings. Call off the wedding. It's not too late."

Her head started to shake back and forth. It felt like a kick in the gut. But the doubt in her eyes spurred him on. If he could be more persuasive, he could convince her. He had to. Their happiness—his and hers—hung in the balance.

"Don't get married just because the plans are in place. You and I are in love. We deserve to be happy."

The sadness in her eyes told him everything. She rested her hand on his shoulder, then leaned forward and kissed him again, their lips meeting in a sweet, tender caress. He wrapped his arms around her and deepened the kiss, determined to convince her. Her arms glided around his neck and she melted against him. Passion flared and his heart soared.

Then he felt her withdraw before their lips even parted. As soon as she drew away, he saw the sadness in her eyes and knew he had lost.

He sucked in a breath.

"I'm sorry, Evan. I'm marrying Brent."

At that, she turned around and stepped off the wooden deck, then rushed past the opening in the trees and toward the house.

His heart sank at the knowledge that he had lost. The woman he loved was going to marry another man.

# Three

Evan followed Crystal as she rushed back to the house, holding the sides of her robe so she wouldn't trip. Renee, who was talking to one of the bridesmaids, broke away and hurried over to intercept Crystal.

"Honey, your lipstick is smeared." Renee opened her small purse and handed Crystal a tissue, lipstick, and a small compact mirror, then turned to Evan and wiped his mouth with a tissue. It came away with dark pink smudges. "Okay, so what's happening? Do you want me to get Brent over here so you can talk?"

"What do you mean?" Crystal asked.

"Look, I've known all along that you have feelings for Evan." Renee ignored Crystal as she shook her head back and forth in denial. "I know you're very good at hiding your emotions, even from yourself, but surely you can't deny how you feel about Evan now. Not after kissing the man less than an hour before your wedding."

"I've kissed lots of people today. It's my wedding day."

Renee snorted. "Yeah, but not lipstick-smearing, leaving-a-guilty-expression-on-your-face passionate kisses."

Crystal's cheeks stained crimson, and she didn't deny her sister's comments. Hope danced through Evan. Could it be that she did have feelings for him?

"Renee, I'm in love with Brent. I have been for years. I'm marrying Brent."

The optimism filling him quickly deflated, as though she'd punched him in the gut.

"Honey, look, are you sure? If you've found out you made a mistake, it's better to do something about it now than—"

"Renee, I need to talk to you."


Crystal glanced toward Brent's sister's voice. Lily stood a few feet away, obviously reluctant to intrude.

"Lily, now's not a good time," Renee said.

"I know, but . . . it's important."

Renee gave Crystal a quick squeeze. "I'll be right back." She walked toward Lily, and they began talking in low voices.

Crystal glanced at Evan, then gazed down at her hands.

"What do you mean he's gone?" Renee glanced toward Crystal, then lowered her voice again.

Crystal's heart clenched at the words, and she watched Renee and Lily confer while she wrung her hands together.

"You're sure?" Renee stared hard at Lily. "Maybe he just took a walk."

Lily shook her head. "His car's gone."

"Well, maybe he—"

Crystal's heart thundered in her chest as she concentrated so she could hear the two women's words, even though they spoke in low murmurs.

"No. I know my brother. He hates to be late. Ever. And with something as important as his own wedding, there's no way he'd leave less than a half hour before the ceremony. It just wouldn't happen."

"So you think he's . . . gone? He's standing up my sister?"

Lily shook her head. "I don't understand it, but . . . He won't answer his cell, he's gone, and so is his car." She shrugged. "I don't know what to say."

Renee patted Lily's shoulder, then both women glanced toward Crystal, their faces somber.

Crystal's mind blanked as Renee approached. She couldn't think. She felt numb.

"Honey . . ." Renee took her hand. It felt hot compared with her own, and . . . hers trembled. "Sweetie, we're not sure where Brent is."

"He probably lent his car to someone," Crystal said. "And right now, he's probably just out for a walk. I'm sure he'll be right back."

Renee glanced at Lily, then back to Crystal. "Okay, look. You go back to the house and get ready. I'll call Bill and see if he knows what's up. I'll send Rachel up to help you get ready."

Crystal nodded and started toward the house. Bill was one of Brent's groomsmen. He would probably know where Brent was. Renee waved at Rachel, who stood near the house. Rachel nodded as Renee pointed to Crystal and lifted her bridesmaid's skirt as she hurried to intercept her.

Crystal gazed at her tense face in the mirror as Rachel finished pinning the headpiece in place, then fussed with the veil. Thirty minutes had passed and she tried to quell the growing sense of dread that things were going to go terribly wrong. Didn't every bride think that on her wedding day?

Surely Renee had tracked down Brent by now. He'd only been out for a walk. That's all. Nothing to be alarmed about. Sure, he was late, but there was a reasonable explanation. She knew there was.

A knock sounded at the door. Crystal jerked around, the motion causing the veil to tug from Rachel's fingers.

"Come in," Crystal called.

The door opened and Renee stepped inside. Lily and Evan followed her in, and Evan closed the door behind them.

"Honey," Renee said softly, "we can't find Brent. He's not answering his cell."

"He's probably just not getting a signal. But he'll be right back." Her head nodded up and down like a bobble-head doll.

Renee squeezed her hand. "Look, honey, we've got

to face the fact that he might not be showing up." She glanced at her watch. "He's already twenty minutes late."

Crystal found it hard to breathe. She clung to Renee. "No. He wouldn't do that to me." She gazed at Renee imploringly. "He loves me."

Renee's eyes glimmered and she pulled Crystal against her, hugging her tightly. "I know, sweetie, I know. I don't know why this is happening, but we'll figure it out." She drew away and gazed at her. "But we have to deal with right now. If he doesn't show up, there'll be no wedding. At least, not today."

Crystal sucked in air, feeling faint.

"Honey, breathe. Everything will be okay."


Evan's chest tightened as he watched Crystal struggling with the news. God damn it, how could Brent abandon her like this? Leaving a woman like Crystal at the altar . . . the guy had to be crazy.

Renee glanced toward him. "Evan, I parked my car over at Georgia's in case anyone needed to run any last minute errands. All the cars here will be blocked in by guests." She handed him her car keys. "Take Crystal over to the Windsor Hotel. Everyone thinks they'll be staying at the Tudor Inn, but I wanted to surprise them with the bridal suite. I've had all her things moved there, so she'll have a change of clothes. Stay there with her until we figure this out."

"No, Renee, I need to stay here," Crystal said.

Renee turned back to Crystal. "No, honey, you go

with Evan. If Brent shows up, I promise I'll call and we'll get everything back on track. Okay?"

Evan put a comforting arm around Crystal's shoulder. "Crystal, we won't be very far. We can get back in no time. I promise."

She gazed up at him, her eyes glistening with unshed tears. Finally, she nodded.

"Evan, I'll give you my cell phone and I'll take Crystal's. The last thing she needs is to get a bunch of phone calls from well-meaning friends. I have the ring tone set to the 'Wedding March' if it's Crystal's number, so you'll know it's me calling."

Evan nodded as he took the tiny pink phone.

"Give me your phone, honey," Renee said to Crystal.

Crystal opened the small white satin bag hanging from her wrist and handed her red phone to her sister.

Renee took her shoulders. "I'm going to wait a half hour. If Brent doesn't show up by then, I'm going to tell the guests that the two of you talked it over and decided to call off the wedding."

Crystal stared at her with wide eyes.

"Good plan, Renee," Evan said.

"I'm not going to have my little sister embarrassed like that," she said through gritted teeth. "All I can say is, when I see that son of a bitch, I'm going to—" She bit back whatever she was going to say and glanced at Crystal. She turned to Evan. "You two should just go."

Ten minutes later, Evan helped fold the rest of Crystal's full skirt into the compact car and closed the door. He hopped in and drove down the dirt driveway that meandered through the woods to the main road. Another ten minutes later, they sped along the highway.

He glanced at Crystal, who simply stared out the side window.

"How are you doing?" he asked.

She simply shook her head and remained silent. He took the ramp to Braker Road, then after a few turns pulled into the parking lot of the sumptuous Windsor Hotel. He drove to the front entrance and a doorman opened Crystal's door and offered his hand. Evan jumped out and hurried to Crystal's side. She looked so lost.

He gave the keys to the doorman. "Can you arrange to have the car parked?"

"Of course, sir." He smiled. "And congratulations."

Crystal wore a wedding dress. Evan was in a tuxedo. Of course the man assumed Evan was the groom. Everyone would assume that.

He took Crystal's elbow and led her into the hotel, then to the reception desk. There was a short lineup, but another staff member, a young woman in a navy suit, approached them.

"Come over here and I'll help you," she said with a smile. "We can't have a new bride and groom standing in line."

She checked her computer and handed them a small folder with a key card, then Evan led Crystal to the elevator. Within moments, they were walking down the eighteenth-floor hallway toward the suite Renee had arranged for Crystal . . . and Brent.

He opened the door and waited while Crystal entered the suite.

"Oh, it's beautiful," she said.


Crystal glanced around as she stepped inside. The place was huge and the furnishings elegant. A large sitting area with a couch and two chairs faced the large window overlooking the river beyond. There were several large fresh flower arrangements around the room that filled the air with a lovely scent. She noticed a door across the room and realized that would be the bedroom. That's where she and Brent would have consummated their marriage tonight if . . . if . . . Her throat constricted.

Like a woman in a trance, she continued across the room, heading for the door. She turned the crystal knob and pushed open the door. Inside, a huge canopied bed dominated the room. And there were more flowers. The bed was turned down, revealing pristine white sheets strewn with red rose petals. She stepped into the room, staring at the bed, her heart twisting. She glanced around and saw her suitcase on a stand against the wall and Brent's on another stand beside hers.

Then she noticed a framed picture on the dresser. An eight-by-ten of the engagement picture taken of her and Brent. It had been used for their wedding announcement. In it, Brent looked so handsome in his gray suit. It made his already broad shoulders look even broader, and his wide smile softened the square line of his jaw. His dark brown hair was so wavy and appealing, and warmth emanated from his brown eyes. Beside him, she looked so happy, beaming at the camera like a new bride.

Like a happy bride.

She gazed at her reflection in the mirror. Not like the morose face she saw staring back at her now. And Brent . . . Oh, God, he was so handsome . . . and the look on his face. So loving. But . . . he didn't really love her. He couldn't. Not after what he had done to her today.

Her heart thundered in her chest, and her dress felt too tight around her. She could barely breathe. She reached behind her and clawed at the zipper until she found the tag, then she ripped it down.

"Crystal?"

She ignored Evan as she raked at the sleeves until she managed to pull them off, then she shoved the dress down past her hips and climbed out of the voluminous skirt. As she skittered away from it, her headpiece tugged on her head since the veil was caught under the skirt of the dress, so she pulled it off, scattering hairpins everywhere.

She scurried to the love seat by the fireplace and perched on the edge. The beautiful marquise-cut diamond on her ring finger caught the sunlight from the window. She held up her hand and stared at the engagement ring she and Brent had picked out together. The symbol of their undying love for each other.

She slid it off her finger and let it drop to the floor.

Then she hugged herself and began to shiver.

———

Evan watched Crystal, his chest constricting at her obvious distress. Still, the sight of her in the skintight white satin basque, which held her breasts up and forward as if offering them, made his body tighten in need. And her long, slender legs in stockings held up by garters, the tops of her creamy white thighs left bare . . .

His heart pounded.

He wanted to hold her and comfort her, but if he got close to her . . . touched her . . . he didn't know how he'd hold himself in check.

Then her tears started to flow, and he sucked in a breath. He sat beside her and tucked his arm around her, his hand curling around her silky smooth arm. He drew her close and she rested her face against his chest. For a long time, he held her gently as she sobbed softly. After a while, when her sobs turned to slow breathing, he scooped her up and carried her to the bed, then laid her down. He pulled off her shoes, then drew the covers over her.

"Don't go." She gazed up at him with puffy eyes.

"I'll stay as long as you like."

"Hold me?"

He nodded and kicked off his shoes, then tossed aside his tuxedo jacket. His white shirt was stained with black mascara, but that didn't matter. He climbed in the bed beside her and wrapped his arms around her. She snuggled against him.

He held her close, reveling in the softness of her body pressed to his. After a while, he could tell by her even breathing that she'd fallen asleep. He hated to see her so unhappy, but he couldn't help thinking that this meant maybe he had a chance with her. And he hated himself for thinking about that right now.

After about a half hour, she murmured softly in her sleep, then shifted restlessly. Her hand bumped against his chest, then she murmured again and her fingers moved along her side.

"Crystal?"

She didn't answer. Since she still seemed to be asleep, he lifted the covers to see what was going on. Her fingers worked at the hooks on the basque as she tried—unsuccessfully—to unfasten them.

Without thinking, he unfastened the long row of hooks. As the white fabric parted, exposing more of her silky flesh, the cadence of his heartbeat increased.

Oh, this was really not a good idea.

Still, he couldn't stop himself. Finally, he unfastened the last hook. She pulled the basque from her body and sighed. At the first glimpse of her naked breasts—round and perfect—he pulled the sheet up again. Along her side, however, he felt the indentation on her skin where the basque had been digging into her. He stroked the skin and she sighed, then leaned back against him.

He couldn't stop thinking about those lovely breasts as he stroked her skin, wishing she would turn around and snuggle against him, yet at the same time praying she wouldn't. Because if she did, it would be sweet torture.

Her breathing settled again, and she seemed to be deep in sleep. He dozed off, then awoke to a movement against him. He wasn't sure how much time had passed, but his grogginess told him he had been fast asleep.

Crystal had turned toward him and settled her head against his chest. He could feel her soft breasts pressed against him through the fabric of his shirt. She nuzzled his chest, then he felt the movement of her fingers. He almost jumped when he realized she was unfastening his shirt buttons.

Oh, God, she probably thought he was Brent.

With great strength of will, he stilled her hands.

"Crystal . . ." He didn't really know what to say, especially since he didn't want to remind her of Brent's abandonment, so he simply trailed off.

He felt her soft cheek brush against his partially bared chest.

"Yes, Evan?" She continued to unfasten his shirt.

"I, uh . . . what are you doing?" Man, that was lame.

# Four

"I've gotten makeup all over your white shirt." Crystal gazed at the sculpted muscles of Evan's chest as she pushed his shirt over his shoulders.

She couldn't help but grin at his reaction. He was trying so hard to be the gentleman and not take advantage of the situation. Maybe *he* wouldn't, but she certainly intended to.

Her heart still ached at the fact that Brent had walked out on her, but right here, right now, she was with a man who wanted her. He had told her so. And then he'd taken care of her in her hour of need.

She tugged his shirt off his arms, then pushed it away. He was a great guy, and he wanted to be with her. And right now, she needed to feel wanted.

She glided her hands down his solid chest, then along the waistband of his pants. When she unfastened the button, he grabbed her hands.

"Crystal, that's probably not a good idea. You—"

She drew her hands free and pushed against his chest until he rolled onto his back, then she prowled over him.

"That's funny. I think it's a great idea."

She rose onto her knees and his eyes widened as his gaze fastened on her naked breasts. His look of avid admiration boosted her confidence. She slid backward and rested on his thighs as she drew down his zipper. The impressive bulge filling his black boxers encouraged her even more. She shifted to the side and pulled his tuxedo pants down to his knees, then stroked over his hard, long erection, anticipating drawing it out and seeing it for the first time. Her nipples swelled and her insides ached with desire.

He kicked away the pants, then arched up against her hand.

"Crystal, we really shouldn't be doing this."

She squeezed the bulge, then reached inside and wrapped her hand around his engorged cock.

"Who says?"

"I—" He groaned as she stroked his length.

She reached for his hands and pressed them to her breasts. He held them reverently as he stared at her in awe. She arched against him, pressing his palms tight to her. Finally, he closed his fingers around her soft mounds. She released his hands and wrapped her fingers around his cock again. He caressed her, sending tingles dancing through her body.

"Oh, Evan, that feels wonderful."

She drew out his cock, so long and hard, and stared at it. The bulbous head looked as though it would fill her mouth nicely, and the thick ridge around the head would drag against her inner walls as he drew back after he thrust deep inside her. The thought sent her head spinning. She leaned forward and licked his tip. He groaned. One of his hands glided through her hair as the other continued to stroke her breast.

Until she swallowed his cockhead whole. He groaned, and his hand slipped from her breast. She licked in a spiral over him, then sucked. His fingers forked through her hair. She took him deep in her mouth, his cock pressing into her throat. She glided away, a restless need rising in her.

She grasped his cock tightly and sat up.

"I want you, Evan." She pushed herself onto her knees and pressed his cock to her opening. The silk of her panties acted as a barrier between them. She stared deep into his eyes. "I want you."

He nodded, as if hypnotized.

"Do we need a condom?" she asked.

"I've . . . uh . . . been tested recently," he said hesitantly, clearly still uncertain about going ahead with this.

She nodded. "I was tested when I started dating Brent." She ignored the pain lancing through her at the thought of her absent fiancé. "I haven't been with anyone since. And I'm on the pill."

He nodded, so she hooked the fingers of her free hand around the crotch of her panties and pulled it aside, then pressed his cockhead to her opening, already slick from her desire to feel him inside her. As soon as she felt his hot, hard flesh against her naked folds, she sank down on him. She sucked in a deep breath, then groaned—an echo to his guttural murmur—as his hard, thick cock pushed into her, filling her deeply. Finally, she sat flush against his hips, his erection fully immersed in her.

Oh, God, he felt so good inside her.

Then she simply stared at him. And he stared at her. Yearning filled his eyes. She felt wanted. Needed. Desired.

"Oh, God, Evan. I want you so much."

His eyes glittered, and just like that, the uncertainty left his face. A low growl rumbled from him and he rolled her over in one swift motion. His groin pinned her to the bed, his cock still filling her. With his hands planted on either side of her head, he smiled down at her.

"Well, now . . ." He grinned as he drew back, his cock dragging against her inner passage and sending excruciatingly delightful pleasure dancing through her. "As it turns out, I want you, too."

At his sharp forward thrust, she gasped. She wrapped her hands around his broad, muscular shoulders. Damn, but she'd never realized how extremely well sculpted his body was.

He drew back and thrust into her again. She tightened around him, pleasure building inside her.

"Oh, Evan."

It felt incredible having his huge cock filling her. The wild sensations made her head swim.

"What is it, Crystal? Do you like this?" He drew back, then thrust forward again.

She nodded, incapable of expressing herself in words.

He drew back again, then hovered there, his cockhead

barely inside her, in danger of slipping free. Oh, God, she wanted him back inside her. Deep. His hard length filling her.

He leaned in close and murmured in her ear.

"I want you to talk to me. Tell me what you want."

"I . . ." She hesitated, trying to articulate what she wanted but failing. She simply needed him inside her.

His gazed locked with hers, and she stared into the forest green depths and concentrated.

"Tell me what you want, love."

*Love.* Her heart melted.

Fiery desire filled his eyes, but with an overriding tenderness.

"I . . . I want you to make love to me."

He nodded in encouragement, but she sensed he didn't want sweet words right now.

"I want you to grind that big cock of yours into me. To drive it in deep. I want you to fuck me so hard, I'll scream your name at the top of my lungs."

His mouth turned up in a broad grin, then he nuzzled her neck.

"Now, was that so hard?"

Before she could answer, he drove deep inside her and she gasped. Then he kept on thrusting, filling her, drawing back, then filling her again. She clung to him as pleasure swept through her, then washed her over the edge of forever.

"Oh, God, Evan. Oh . . ." She sucked in air, then moaned. "Oh, Evan. You're making me . . ." She gasped again.

"I'm making you what, love? Tell me." His intense gaze held hers as he continued to plunge into her.

Pleasure quivered through her, tickling her senses. She could barely think straight.

"Come. Oh, God, you're making me . . ." Joy swelled through her. "Ah . . . come!" The last word broke into a long moan as an orgasm erupted through her.

Evan groaned and drove deep into her. She could feel him pulse inside her. They clung to each other, riding the waves of bliss together.

Finally, his body relaxed and she sighed in contentment. He nuzzled her neck, then rolled to her side, gazing at her with glittering eyes. She smiled, then he captured her lips in a sweet, lingering kiss.

She snuggled against him and lay in silence, not willing to threaten their afterglow with words that might drag them abruptly back to reality.

Evan couldn't believe it. Crystal's soft body was pressed tightly against him, both of them still hot and slick from their passionate lovemaking. He didn't want this moment to end. He drew his arm tighter around her, reveling in her warmth and the delicate scent of vanilla in her hair.

The sound of a cell phone ring tone—the "Wedding March"—broke the silence. Crystal tensed in his arms, probably at the reminder that this was her wedding day and her groom had abandoned her.

He snatched up the pink cell phone from the bedside table.

"Hello, Renee," he said.

"How's she doing?" Renee asked.

"Okay, considering."

He glanced down at Crystal, and she nodded and reached for the phone.

"Hi, Renee." Crystal drew away from him and sat up, tucking the sheet around her body. "Uh, no, not here." She paused. "No, really, I'm fine going out somewhere." She glanced at Evan. "Yeah, we'll find it."

Crystal hung up. "She wants to meet with us. She suggested coffee at a bistro a couple of streets over. Is that okay with you?"

"Of course." Except that it meant they both had to leave this bed.

She stood up, pulling the sheet with her, and shuffled to one of the suitcases on a stand against the wall. She pulled out some clothes, then headed into the bathroom. Just before she closed the door, she stuck her head into the room again.

"Go ahead and grab some clothes from Brent's suitcase."

Once she closed the door, Evan stood up and approached the dark gray suitcase. He rifled through it and pulled out a pair of jeans and a striped blue cotton shirt. He didn't like the idea of wearing Brent's clothes, but he couldn't go out in his tuxedo.

Ten minutes later, they walked along the street in the late afternoon sunlight.

"There it is," Crystal said, pointing to the blue-and-white sign indicating the Blue Heron Bistro.

He opened the door for her, and she stepped inside.

Renee waved at them from a table by the window. They sat down and Crystal took a sip of the iced tea Renee had waiting for her.

"How are you doing, honey?" Renee asked, gazing at her with concern.

Crystal shrugged. She couldn't lie and say she was fine. Even if she could, Renee would see right through her. Renee patted Crystal's hand. It was amazing how such a small gesture from her big sister made her feel so cared for.

Renee glanced at Evan. "So, have you been keeping our girl entertained?"

Crystal felt Evan stiffen beside her, and she stifled a giggle. "He's been wonderful."

Renee glanced at her and raised an eyebrow. "Really?"

Their gazes locked, and Crystal knew Renee had figured out exactly what had happened between them.

"That's great," Renee continued. "So listen, about the trip."

Crystal's chest constricted. She didn't want to think about her honeymoon. The one she was supposed to go on with the man who loved her, but who obviously *didn't* love her or he wouldn't have betrayed her. But at the same time, the thought of losing her dream trip sent her gut churning.

"I think you should still go," Renee said.

"How can I go on my honeymoon now?"

"Well, you're not thinking of giving up the trip you've been looking forward to for so long just because of that jerk, are you?"

Crystal stared at her hands. Damn it.

"Anyway, getting away from everything would be the best thing for you right now."

Crystal shook her head. "I don't want to go alone."

"I don't think you should go alone." Renee opened her purse and pulled out a piece of paper and unfolded it. "I rebooked the two tickets for this evening. I thought it would be better if you left right away. Why wait?"

Renee was a travel agent and had handled all the arrangements. Crystal took the paper and glanced at the flight information.

She gazed at her sister. "Are you going to go with me?" How had her sister arranged to take off two weeks from work on such short notice?

"No. I had something else in mind." Renee glanced toward Evan. "Um, do you think you could give us a minute?"

"Sure." Evan stood up. "I'll go out for a walk."

Once he was gone, Renee turned her gaze back to Crystal. "Look, it's clear that you two have some major chemistry going on. What's wrong with getting away from the everyday routine and seeing where this thing between you goes?"

"Well, maybe because I was supposed to get married today," Crystal said in a dry tone.

"But you didn't. And your fiancé turned out to be a rat fink, so don't let some misplaced sense of propriety get in the way of finding true happiness."

Crystal shifted uncomfortably. "Renee, you're getting carried away."

Renee drummed her fingers on the table. "Maybe, but sometimes you really need a push, and I don't want to see you ignore this chance." She leaned forward. "Honey, forget happily-ever-after. Just think about having a wild, sexy time with a great-looking guy who thinks the world of you. That's enough for now."

Her heart constricted. "But . . . he said he loved me."

"In the hotel suite?"

"No, before the wedding. When we went for a walk. If I ask him to go away with me, maybe he'll read too much into it. Maybe he'll assume I'm ready for happily-ever-after with him."

"Now look who's getting carried away. He knows what just happened, too. He knows you need time to sort things out. Don't push him away because he told you how he feels about you. It's so rare to find a guy who will express his feelings."

Crystal sat back in her chair. The thought of spending the next two weeks moping around her apartment filled her with dread, and she really didn't want to give up her trip. The idea of enjoying those beautiful white beaches and azure water with Evan at her side made her heart thrum. Actually, thinking of making love with him on the soft white sand—or in the big king-size bed in the luxury villa—made her heart thump even faster.

Evan was a self-employed consultant and had a great deal of flexibility in his schedule. He could probably take the time off.

Oh, God, she was actually considering this.

# Five

"Renee thinks I should still go on my honeymoon trip," Crystal said as she walked beside Evan on their way back to the hotel.

"So she mentioned. And it's a good idea. Getting away for a while would be good for you."

They stopped at the curb, waiting for the light to turn green so they could cross the street.

"Yeah, that's what she thinks, too. And I don't really want to go back to San Diego and hang around at home." People at the office would hear about what had happened pretty quickly, since she had invited a few of her work friends to the wedding.

And at some point, she'd run into Brent again. Maybe he'd even stop by to explain what had happened or to see how she was doing, and she wasn't ready to face that anytime soon.

Evan nodded. "You need to get away from your usual environment entirely. Is Renee going with you?"

The light turned green and they started across the road.

"No, actually, she suggested I . . ." She hesitated, unsure how to ask him.

"What did she suggest?"

"She suggested that I invite you."

His expression didn't change. "Really. And what did you say?"

They approached the hotel entrance and the doorman opened the door for them. As they crossed the lobby, she sent him a sidelong glance.

"I told her that I didn't want to give you the wrong impression."

"And that would be?"

"That I'm ready to move forward with a relationship. Especially after . . . what you said . . . before the wedding."

They stepped into a waiting elevator and the doors closed with just the two of them inside.

"That I love you," Evan said.

It was the first time they had talked about his proclamation of love since he'd made it. They hadn't really dealt with it then, and now things had changed. Drastically. But that didn't mean she could just accept his love and move forward. She needed time to figure things out.

He took her hand and turned to face her. "Crystal, I understand that you just had your whole world pulled out from under you. You need time to adjust. To think things through." His fingertips stroked the back of her hand, sending tingles through her. "Of course, I hope that you'll consider giving me a chance, but I know that will take time." He smiled. "And if you decide to invite me, I'll be happy to go. Thrilled, in fact. But I won't assume that means anything more than that you'd like a friend along. Someone to help you get through this." He squeezed her hand. "I'd like to be that friend."

She nodded. She wanted him to be that friend, too. Because she knew she could depend on him. And she wasn't kidding herself at all about the fact that she'd love to have a wild, passionate fling with him. The sex this afternoon had been stupendous, and she wanted more of the same.

Was that selfish of her? To want this man to put his feelings on hold to satisfy her whim?

He smiled and kissed the back of her hand. "Well, don't keep me in suspense. Am I being invited or what?"

"Evan, I can't promise anything. Somehow it doesn't seem fair to—"

Suddenly she found herself in his arms, his lips moving on hers. His tongue swept into her mouth and seared her with his passion. Then he gazed down at her, his green eyes warm.

"Life is rarely fair." He grinned. "But I must say, in this instance, the benefits far outweigh any negatives. And I think taking a vacation with you can only work in my favor. Because, gorgeous, with two weeks to work my magic on you, I think you might just be a convert by the end."

Her heart thumped in her chest and she sucked in air. He was probably right.

"I can't make any promises."

The elevator stopped and the doors opened.

"The only promise I'd like you to make is that you'll keep an open mind," he said. "Deal?"

She nodded and he captured her lips again.

"Great. Now, let's go get ready for the honeymoon."


Brent opened his eyes to sunlight glaring in his face. He sat up, and his head felt as if it was cracking open. Some God-damned bird twittered outside, sending the pain up several notches. He shoved back the hair hanging in his eyes and stood up.

Damn. His knees felt rubbery, and his head throbbed even more. He dropped back onto the bed again, wondering just how many drinks he'd had last night. He raked his hand through his hair. Clearly, too damn many.

He gritted his teeth as the bird continued to sing. How could anybody or anything be so freaking happy on a miserable day like today?

Sure, the sun shone brightly and the sky was clear of clouds, but . . . damn it, right now he should be on his honeymoon with the woman he loved, not alone in a hotel along the highway suffering from a mega-hangover.

His heart compressed at the memory of Crystal in Evan's arms, the two locked in a passionate kiss. God damn, how could his best friend steal away the woman he loved? And in the final hour before the wedding. And Crystal . . . how could she just fall into his arms like that?

It didn't make any sense.

It would never make any sense to him.

With every drink last night, he'd hoped to understand. He stood up, slowly this time.

That wasn't exactly true. He'd been trying to ease the stinging pain. To wash away the agony in his heart.

But it hadn't worked. Of course it hadn't.

The scene at the lake still remained burned into his memory. As he'd stepped past the trees into the clearing near Crystal's favorite spot, he had seen Crystal and Evan kissing passionately. He'd frozen on the spot, not believing what he was seeing. But he knew he must have been misreading the situation, convincing himself it was just a congratulatory kiss. From his vantage point, he hadn't been able to see Crystal's face, but he'd heard Evan's words, and those words still rang through his mind.

*Crystal, you obviously share my feelings. Call off the wedding. It's not too late.*

*Don't get married just because the plans are in place. You and I are in love. We deserve to be happy.*

At that point, Crystal had fallen into Evan's arms again, kissing him with so much passion, it shocked Brent to the core.

The sight of the woman he loved kissing his best friend, obviously ready to run away with him, had destroyed him. He'd turned around and gone straight back to the house where he'd stayed the night before, grabbed his overnight bag, and leaped in the car. His sister, Lily, had still been in the shower. He hadn't taken time to write a note, and he sure hadn't wanted to face her. He'd just started driving. Generally heading toward home. He'd been too tired and distraught to make the whole thirteen-hour drive back to San Diego, so he'd pulled off the highway at a hotel partway. Only when he'd walked into his room had he remembered it was the same hotel he, Crystal, and Evan had stayed at on the way to Crystal's parents' place a week ago. At that realization, he'd headed straight to the bar.

And now he was suffering the aftereffects.

He gazed in the mirror and saw his dark brown hair sticking out in all directions. He ran his fingers through it, smoothing it down a little. He still wore his tuxedo, at least the shirt and pants. The rumpled jacket lay strewn on the floor, having slipped from the back of the chair he'd tossed it on last night. The tie wasn't anywhere to be seen.

He picked up the jacket and hung it on a hanger, then unzipped his overnight bag and pulled out his jeans and a cotton shirt, then tossed them on the bed. He pulled off the rumpled tuxedo pants and shirt and tossed them on the bed, then shed his boxers.

In the bathroom, he turned on the shower and waited until the water ran hot, then stepped under it. He scrubbed his skin with soap and washed his hair, then rinsed off. Where was Crystal right now? Somewhere in Evan's arms?

After towel drying himself, he combed his hair and brushed his teeth, then glared at the sap staring back at him in the mirror.

How could Crystal turn her back on him and everything they meant to each other to take off with Evan less than an hour before their wedding? How could she just walk away? And why then? With all their family and friends waiting for them?

He strode back into the bedroom and pulled on a clean pair of boxers, then his jeans and shirt. The more he thought about it in the sober light of day, the more he wondered at what had actually happened. Could he have misinterpreted what he'd seen?

Brent's gut twisted as he remembered seeing Crystal in Evan's embrace, her arms gliding around his neck, her body melting against his. He couldn't believe his so-called best friend had made a move on Crystal.

Damn, he and Evan had been through so much together over the past twenty years. His heart ached as he remembered when Evan had sat up with him all night after his father had died four years ago, helping him through the pain. How Evan had loaned him money when he'd lost his job and started falling behind on bills and rent.

And when Brent had had his heart broken for the first time when he was nineteen, Evan had been the one to pick up the pieces and assure him there would be other women in his life. That he would eventually find the woman of his heart. The woman he was meant to be with.

That woman was Crystal, and now . . .

His hands clenched into fists. How could Evan steal her away from him?

Damn, he had always counted his blessings to have a friend like Evan. Until now. God damn it, how could Evan betray him like this?

And how could Crystal?

He raked his hand through his hair. Despite all of it,

though, maybe Brent shouldn't have walked away. At the very least, he should have confronted her. Made her tell him face-to-face that she wanted to end it.

His chest constricted and he slumped into the armchair. But he didn't want it to end. He loved her. God help him, he loved her more than life itself.

His hands clenched around the armrests. So what the hell was wrong with him? Why didn't he fight for her? If she'd given her heart to Evan, Brent would win it back again. He loved her. He would convince her all over again that he was the man she wanted to spend her life with.

He glanced at the clock and realized the flight they'd booked to the Cayman Islands for their honeymoon would be leaving in less than an hour and it was pretty likely Crystal would be on it. She'd been talking about the trip for months. He was sure she wouldn't give it up.

Would she talk Renee into going with her? His chest tightened. Or would she take Evan?

He picked up the phone and, since Crystal probably wouldn't talk to him, he dialed Renee's cell number.

# Six

As Evan closed the door of his private vacation villa, Crystal dropped her purse on the plush carpet and let go of the handle on her carry-on, then slid off her sandals.

"According to the brochures, there's a private pool out back," she said.

He watched as she shrugged her short-sleeved jacket from her shoulders and let it fall to the carpet as she walked into the living room. The aching tiredness from the long night of travel melted away at the sight of her unzipping her dress and shedding it, too. He plunked down the luggage and followed her, enjoying the sway of her nearly naked behind as she sauntered through the house in only her bra and panties. He followed her into a large, bright kitchen with ceramic tiled floors. Off the kitchen was a large sunroom that overlooked the huge, beautifully landscaped, and very private backyard. Bushes surrounded the yard, and tropical flowers added bright color to the setting. A swimming pool glimmered in the sunlight. Beyond that, the yard descended and the ocean could be seen over the lush green foliage.

Crystal grinned over her shoulder as she tossed aside her bra, then shimmied out of her panties. She grabbed the handle of the patio door and slid it open. Evan's gaze lingered on her delightful ass as it swayed back and forth. He followed her into the backyard, shedding his own clothes as he went.

Stark naked, she dove into the water. A moment later, her head broke through the surface and she wiped the water from her eyes.

"The water's beautiful. Come on in." She grinned.

He could see her bare breasts bobbing in the water just below the surface. He tossed aside his boxers and dove in after her. The water was warm, probably about eighty-five degrees. She swam toward him, then tangled her arms around his neck and kissed him. His groin ached at the feel of her delicate lips on his and her soft breasts crushed against his chest. They both sank as they kissed passionately. He wrapped an arm around her waist and drew her to the side of the pool where he could hold on.

Joy careened through him at the feel of her naked body pressed to his and the knowledge that the two of them would be here, alone, for two glorious weeks together.

She grinned, then pushed herself below the water. Her hand wrapped around his swelling cock, then he felt her mouth cover him. The feel of his cockhead nestled in her hot mouth made him groan. God, she was a sexy, exciting woman. Her fingers found his testicles and she stroked as she began to suck on him. His groin tightened and he stroked her hair as she devoured him with her mouth. Finally, she drew away and came up for air.

"Maybe this will be easier." He pushed himself onto the side of the pool, his legs dangling in the water.

She pushed herself up and hooked her arms over his knees.

"Mmm. Yes, this is perfect." She took his cock in her mouth again and teased the tip with her tongue. Then she licked downward until she reached the base. Her hand stroked his balls and she nipped one with her lips, then licked it. A second later, it disappeared into her mouth.

"Oh, baby, that feels so good."

She prodded it with her tongue, teasing and stroking, then sucked lightly. He stroked her hair, reveling in the delightful sensations. His ball slipped free and she licked his cock again. Licking and kissing, she moved up and down its length. One hand wrapped around him while the other caressed his testicles, then she stroked up and down his cock. He felt so full and ready to burst. She covered his cock and swallowed him deep, opening her throat until he filled her to the base. He twitched at the feel of her hot mouth and throat surrounding him.

"Baby, I'm going to come any minute."

She bobbed up and down, her hand wrapped around his base. He swelled even more and his groin tightened. Just before he burst, she withdrew but continued stroking his shaft with her hand. A white fountain burst forward and arced into the pool. Crystal laughed in delight while he rode the wave of pleasure.

When he finished, he sighed and smiled at her. "You are great at that." He leaned forward and kissed her. "Now it's your turn."

He pulled her from the water and set her down beside him, then he slipped into the pool and positioned himself in front of her, resting his elbows on the stone deck. He pressed her knees wide, then smiled at the sight of her slick, clean-shaven pussy. He leaned forward and licked it. She sighed and lay back. He pressed the folds open with his thumbs, then stroked his fingertip over the little button nestled in the flesh.

"Ohhh." She stroked her breasts, which set his cock twitching.

He licked her slit, then teased her clitoris with the tip of his tongue. She moaned. He licked and sucked, watching her stroke her breasts, delighting in the sight. She pinched her hard nipples. He reached upward and cupped one breast, then teased her hard nipple, squeezing it between his thumb and index finger.

She arched her pelvis upward and he pushed his tongue against her button, then he sucked deeply. She moaned. Her accelerated breathing told him she was close. He tweaked her nipple again as he licked and sucked. She gasped, then moaned loudly as she came. His cock grew with need.

Finally, she dropped back and sighed. "That was great." She pushed herself up on her elbows, then sat up. "But it's not enough." She pushed herself into the water and grabbed his cock in her hand. She leaned her face close to his. "Now fuck me."

She pulled his cockhead to her opening. He wrapped his hands around her hips and pulled her against him, driving his hard cock into her. She hung on to the side so they wouldn't sink. He pushed forward, trying to drive into her again, but it didn't really work. He pressed her into the corner, then grabbed the sides of the pool with both hands and drove forward, gliding deep inside her.

"Oh, yeah." Her eyes were bright as she gazed at him.

He couldn't believe he was here, in this tropical paradise, making love to Crystal, the woman of his dreams. Not two days ago, he was sure his chances with her were virtually zero.

He drove in again, and again. She clung to him.

"Oh, God, I'm coming." She moaned as she hung on to his shoulders. Her passage squeezed tight around him.

He watched her face contort in ecstasy, loving every second of it. Loving the fact that he could bring her such pleasure.

When she finished, she flopped her head onto his chest. "Mmm. That was incredible." She gazed up at him. "But you didn't come."

He chuckled and kissed the top of her head. "Well, it was a little too soon after the last time."

"So that means you're just giving up?" She nuzzled his neck and his cock twitched inside her. Her hand stroked across his chest and she tweaked his nipple. "After all, your gigantic cock is still deep inside me." Her vagina tightened around his cock, sending pleasure pulsing through him. "It's so long and hard."

She wrapped her legs around him, pulling his erection

deeper inside her. She tightened her passage again as she drew back a little, then pushed forward again.

God, the little imp knew how to keep a man turned on. She pulsed forward and back until he felt his groin tighten. She caressed her breast and tweaked the nipple. Her head fell back and she moaned.

"Oh, God, you feel so good inside me. You're so big and hard. So incredibly long." She arched forward, taking him deep. "Oh," she whimpered. Then she moaned.

He quivered inside, then he pulled her tight against him as his cock erupted inside her. The pleasure of his sweet release washed through him. He held her close, his fingers tangled in her long hair. She sighed, then smiled up at him.

"That was fun."

He laughed, then captured her lips in a passionate kiss. This was going to be one hell of a vacation.

Brent pulled up in front of the villa beside the white car sitting in the driveway and turned off the engine, glad to finally end his journey. The sun had already set a while ago, and it was dark. He hadn't been able to get a flight until seven this morning, so he'd driven back to San Diego to pack a bag rather than flying out of Sacramento, then he'd traveled for over twelve hours to get here. After getting his luggage, then the rental car, and finding his way here, it was past nine. Damn, he was exhausted. All he wanted to do was climb into bed and sleep, but before he could do that, he had to talk to Crystal.

He raked his hand through his hair. What was she going to say when he showed up unannounced? And as much as he wanted her in his life, his heart still ached at the fact that she'd betrayed him for Evan.

Part of him shouted that this was a lousy idea and that he should drive back to the airport and fly home right now. But in his heart, he knew he couldn't do that. He loved Crystal, and he had to find a way to make things right between them.

Ah, damn. He stared at the front door, lit by a light on either side of the entryway. Whatever awaited him behind that door, he had to face it head-on. He had to convince Crystal that she was meant to be with him.

He got out of the car and strode to the door, then knocked. After a few moments of waiting, he knocked again. He heard someone on the other side of the door, then the door pulled open. Crystal stood before him in a turquoise bathing suit, a sheer floral sarong wrapped around her hips, her long dark brown hair damp and cascading over her shoulders.

Her blue eyes widened, but the surprise immediately flashed to anger.

"Brent, what are you doing here?"

"May I come in?"

She hesitated but finally stepped aside to let him in.

"Crystal, who is it?" Evan walked into the room, then stopped dead when he saw Brent. "Oh."

Pain and anger surged through Brent, and he had to resist the rush of adrenaline urging him to stride across the room and punch his ex–best friend in the face. He turned back to Crystal.

"I had to talk to you. I realize I shouldn't have just walked away the way I did."

Crystal crossed her arms over her chest. "You think?"

He gazed at her flashing eyes and wondered why she was angry at him, but he stayed focused on his purpose. "That's why I'm here. To talk about what happened. To find out your side of the story."

Her eyes blazed brighter. "*My* side of the story? You're the one who didn't show up for our wedding. You . . ." She sucked in a deep breath, then began to pace. "You abandoned me!"

His heart clenched at the pain in her voice. "Aren't you forgetting the part where Evan told you he's in love with you, then you threw yourself into his arms and kissed him passionately?"

She stopped pacing and stared at him with wide eyes. Then guilt washed across her face and she tore her gaze from him.

"I saw the whole thing," he said.

She glanced at Evan—who refused to look in Brent's direction—then back to Brent. "So that's why you left." She started wringing her hands together. "Oh, damn." She sat down, perching on the end of the couch. "It's true. Evan did tell me he loved me, but"—she gazed up at Brent—"you must have missed the part where I told him I was going to marry *you*!"

Hope soared in him. "So you're telling me you're not in love with Evan?"

At the look in her eyes, his hope came crashing down. He shook his head and glared at Evan, then back to her. "So you were going to marry me even though you have feelings for him?"

"Brent, I didn't really know my feelings for Evan until he said something." She gazed down at her hands, folded in her lap. "I knew I was attracted to him, and I always felt guilty about that, but I figured that's all it was. I ignored it." She gazed at him again. "But I did know I was in love with you. Of course I was still going to marry you."

She *was* in love with him.

"And now?" he asked. "Are you saying you have feelings for Evan now?"

"When you left, Renee handled telling the guests what happened. She had Evan take me to the hotel so I wouldn't have to face everyone. Evan helped me through the most difficult hours of my life after you abandoned me."

Brent's heart clenched at the vulnerability in her eyes. Oh, God, he hadn't realized how much he'd hurt her. And those desperate hours after being left alone at the altar, good old Evan had been there to pick up the pieces. Even if Crystal hadn't loved Evan before, clearly she thought she did now.

"Crystal, I'm sorry. My emotions got the best of me. I realize that now. I shouldn't have walked away. That's why I'm here. I love you. I just want to make things right again."

# Seven

Crystal frowned and glanced at Evan. The questioning look in his eyes, mixed with a sense of hopelessness, tore at her heart. Evan loved her. And she knew Brent loved her.

She loved Brent, too, but she also had strong feelings for Evan. Feelings that could well be love. She just needed time to figure it out. To deny those feelings so she could marry Brent and pretend nothing had happened just wouldn't work.

Yet, knowing that Brent hadn't simply changed his mind, hadn't just walked away callously, meant something.

But he had walked away.

"Look, Brent. The fact that you left—"

"But I explained that," he appealed.

"Yes, but you did leave. If you really loved me—"

"I do."

She held up her hand. "If you really loved me, and were totally committed to making this relationship work, then you would have stayed. You would have talked to me, not just run away as soon as things went a little off track." She stood up and walked toward him, staring hard into his eyes. "You should have talked to me." She wrapped her arms around herself. "If we'd gotten married . . . how do I know that you wouldn't just bail at the first sign of trouble?"

Just as Gary had. Her ex-husband had never even been willing to talk about their problems, let alone try to work through them, and when she'd tried to discuss them, he'd called her a nag.

He'd even suggested that her attraction to Brent had led to the eventual breakup of their marriage. But that couldn't be. She'd never acted on that attraction. She'd never even known Gary had noticed it. But obviously she'd been wrong about that.

Now she found herself in the same situation, even though she'd done everything she could to avoid it. But, damn it, it wasn't her fault. She hadn't done anything wrong.

Except that she'd kissed Evan—passionately—and less than an hour before she was to walk down the aisle. She drew her shoulders back. But it was Brent who'd walked away.

"Crystal, that's not fair."

"Really? Why not?"

Brent stared back at her but said nothing. Her heart thundered in her chest as the silence hung between them.

"Crystal, I love you. And I still want to marry you. The fact that I'm here should tell you that I am willing to fight for our relationship. That's why I flew across a continent to find you." He walked toward her, then stood in front of her, gazing into her eyes. "Do you still love me?"

"I . . ." Her chest tightened. "Of course I do."

"Then tell me you'll marry me."

She shook her head. "I . . . can't. You just waltz back here and tell me I should forget everything that's happened since Saturday—since . . . our wedding day—and expect me to just marry you, despite the fact that you left me at the altar?"

"But if you still love me . . ."

She shook her head, then stood up and started pacing again. "I need time." Her hands clenched at her sides. "I need to think."

She strode down the hall and went into the bedroom, then closed the door behind her. Thoughts and emotions collided within her as she walked to the window and gazed out over the ocean, then took a deep breath.


Evan watched Crystal stride away, then turned his gaze back to Brent to find himself staring into the piercing brown eyes of his friend. Or rather ex-friend, from the look on Brent's face.

"How the hell could you do this to me? I thought you were my friend."

Evan felt as though he'd been kicked in the gut. "I am."

Brent's fists clenched. "You have a fucking lousy way of showing it."

"I'm sorry about the way this worked out. I really am."

"Why don't I believe you? You stole Crystal from me right before our wedding. Now she's here with *you* on the honeymoon. It seems to have worked out pretty well for you."

"She's only here with me because you didn't show up for the wedding," Evan shot back.

Brent took a step toward Evan, his eyes blazing. "I didn't show up for the wedding because I believed she'd already decided to run off with *you*."

Evan sucked in a deep breath, realizing this was only making things worse. He took a step back and held up his hands. "Brent, look, we both made some mistakes."

"So you admit you made a mistake?"

"Only in waiting so long to tell Crystal how I felt about her."

Brent glared at him. "Some fucking friend you are."

"Just hear me out." Evan leaned against the back of the couch. "I've had feelings for Crystal for a long time, but I suppressed them. She was your woman."

"Damn right. So why the hell did you change your mind?"

"Mainly because those initial feelings of attraction turned into something deeper, until I finally realized I was in love with her." He wiped his clammy hands on his shorts. "If you two got married, I knew I could never keep being friends with you, feeling about her the way I do. It would be too difficult. I also started wondering if maybe she had feelings for me. I thought I'd sensed something between us."

"Fuck, did you hit on Crystal before?"

Evan shook his head. "No, nothing like that, but occasionally I'd see her looking at me and . . . I don't know, it just seemed—"

Brent scowled. "So my girlfriend gives you a sidelong glance and you think you have the right to tell her you love her?"

"Damn it, Brent." Evan pushed himself from the couch and paced across the carpet. "Try and see it from my point of view. I was in love with her. There was a chance she returned those feelings, but momentum was carrying her forward to marry you."

"Momentum?" Brent's sharp voice slashed through Evan.

"I know she cares about you, but what if it's me she really loves? Don't you want her to be happy?"

"Don't give me that crap. Of course I want her to be happy. And I'm the man who'll make her happy."

Evan stopped pacing and faced Brent again. "Look, I just had to give it a shot, okay? My happiness is important, too."

"More important than mine?"

"Of course not. But if she was in love with you, she would have said no to me."

"Which she did."

"That's true. And if you two had gotten married, it would have ended there. I would have known she was with the man she truly loved. But . . ."

"But what?" Brent said with narrowed eyes.

"But then you left and it's become clear Crystal does have feelings for me. Now it's a matter of letting her figure out which one of us she wants to spend the rest of her life with."

Crystal heard Brent's and Evan's raised voices through the door but couldn't tell what they were saying. She wrung her hands together. What a mess.

A few minutes later, a tap sounded at the door.

"Crystal, it's Evan. May I come in?"

Poor Evan. How must he be feeling about all this?

"Yes, come in." She turned to face the door as he stepped inside.

"So . . . how are you doing?"

She shook her head. "I don't know. Confused. Uncertain. I need time to process everything that's happened."

"I assume with Brent here . . ." He gazed at his suitcase standing on the rack next to hers. "Maybe I should sleep in the guest room."

Oh, God, the thought of sleeping in here with Evan, and Brent in the next room . . . it didn't seem right. Damn, what a mess.

She nodded. "Thank you for understanding." Oh, damn, did Evan think Brent would be sleeping in here with her? Did Brent? "Um . . . there's only one guest room, and . . ."

"If you're worried about Brent, he's already crashed in the sunroom."

She nodded. "So the two of you talked?"

"A little. Then he glared daggers at me and stormed

off. He found the couch in the sunroom and grabbed the spare bedding from the cupboard." Evan leaned against the dresser. "I think we have some tense times ahead. Crystal, I'm sorry I caused this whole mess. But I've got to say, no matter what happens between Brent and me, I'm glad I told you how I feel. I know you're going to have a hard decision ahead, but . . . I'm still hoping you'll choose me."

She pursed her lips and nodded. She knew once she calmed down, she should choose Brent. Now that she knew Brent hadn't walked out on her because he didn't love her, that he'd done it as a reaction to feeling betrayed, she had to view everything in a whole new light. Brent was the sensible, logical choice. He was her fiancé. They'd been in love for years. They'd been planning the wedding for months. Everything pointed to that decision.

But he shouldn't have walked out on her. The fact that he would do that did not bode well for the health of their marriage.

She glanced at Evan. Concern for her burned in his eyes. The time they'd spent together the past two days had forced her to take another look at her feelings for him. And now she could no longer lie to herself. She could no longer deny she was falling in love with Evan.

Even though she had never fallen out of love with Brent.


Crystal lay staring at the ceiling in the dark room, fully aware of the fact that Evan slept in the room right next to hers, and Brent was asleep on the couch in the sunroom, overlooking the pool.

Damn. If everything had gone as planned—if her life hadn't been sent totally off balance by Evan's proclamation of love on her wedding day—she and Brent would be married now. Both snuggled up in this bed, his strong arms around her.

He should be in this bed with her, holding her . . . making love to her. It should be their honeymoon.

If only things hadn't gone so terribly wrong.

But would that really have been such a good thing? Images of Evan's face, of his poignant lovemaking, sent her insides aquiver. God, Evan loved her. He'd loved her for a long time. And she'd ignored her own feelings for him. Denied them. Because she loved Brent.

Her heart constricted. But she did have feelings for Evan. Confusing, tumultuous, *passionate* feelings.

Oh, God, the walls seemed to be closing in on her, the darkness pressing around her.

She pushed aside the covers, slid on her slippers, and padded down the hall to the kitchen. She opened the fridge and stared inside for something to drink. Her mouth was so dry. She pulled out a bottle of water and poured it into a glass, then sipped it while she gazed out the window at the swimming pool. The water glittered in the moonlight.

Memories of her lovemaking with Evan by the pool filled her mind. Now she felt guilty about it, but she had no reason to feel guilty. She'd thought Brent had left her for good. In fact, she felt anger well up. Brent had walked away. He had no reason to be angry with her for what had happened between her and Evan.

But he probably wasn't angry. He was hurt. Because he loved her.

Damn, damn, damn. This was such a mess.

She gulped back the rest of the water and set her glass in the sink, then gripped the counter.

The bottom line was that she did still love Brent. That hadn't changed just because of the messed-up wedding day. Her eyes welled with tears when she remembered how he'd taken her to a lovely getaway for the weekend and knelt in front of her and proposed. She'd laughed in joy and thrown her arms around him. He'd spun her around and they'd laughed together. Then he'd made love to her in front of the fireplace, a roaring fire heating their naked bodies.

She put down her glass and walked to the doorway of the large sunroom off the kitchen. The moon shining in the window cast enough light that she could see him stretched out on the couch. Her heart ached at the sight of him.

Quietly, she stepped into the room. She sat on the armchair kitty-corner to the couch and gazed at his strong, handsome face glazed in moonlight.


Brent felt her presence. Somehow, he knew Crystal was in the room with him. He opened his eyes and glanced around. She sat on the chair near the couch, only a couple of feet from him.

"Crystal?"

Her wide eyes glimmered in the moonlight. "Brent, I . . ." Her words choked off and she sucked in a deep breath.

"What is it, sweetheart?" he encouraged.

"I thought you'd left me for good. I thought . . ." She sucked in a breath again. "I thought you . . . didn't love me anymore."

Her words wrenched his gut. He sat up and took her hand. "Oh, God, sweetheart, no. That would never happen." He gazed at her, his eyes glittering in the moonlight. "Remember what I said the night I proposed?"

They had taken a winery tour in the Napa Valley and stayed at a quaint little bed-and-breakfast Crystal had heard great things about from a friend.

Crystal's lips turned up in a tenuous smile and she nodded. "You said you'd do anything for me—to show how much you loved me. And you hoped to show me that as time went on." She gazed down at her hand, then her smile faded. "Then you asked me to marry you."

He drew her hand to his mouth. The feel of her soft palm against his lips sent heat thrumming through his body. He pushed himself from the couch and knelt in front of her.

"I love you so much." He stared at her, willing her to believe him. "I will love you forever." He cupped her cheeks, then drew her closer and captured her lips. "I'll never walk out on you again."

She hesitated at first, then her arms wrapped around him and she returned the kiss, gliding her tongue into his mouth and undulating against his. His groin tightened and he pulled her tighter against him, her breasts crushed against his chest, her nipples thrusting into him as they hardened into pebbles.

Oh, God, he wanted her. To feel the warmth of her body wrapped around him again. To see love shining in her eyes. For him.

He wanted to feel what it was like to make love to her again. Wanted to experience making love in their luxury resort villa, as they'd dreamed of for so many happy months while planning their wedding. Starting their new life together.

Their lips parted and he gazed at her.

"Oh, God, Crystal. I've missed you. I thought I'd lost you."

# Eight

The pain in Brent's warm brown eyes reached deep into Crystal's soul. She surged forward, kissing him with abandon.

"Brent, I love you, too."

Her body ached for him. These past couple of days with Evan had been wonderful, but . . . She wanted everything to be as it was. To feel this man, whom she loved so dearly, making love to her again.

Confusing, tumultuous emotions swirled through her, but she grabbed Brent's hand and stood up, then tugged him across the room with her.

Brent wasn't sure exactly what was going on in Crystal's head, but he wasn't going to let this opportunity get away from him. He wanted her to tell him that everything was back to the way it used to be and that she'd still marry him, but the confusion of emotions swirling across her face told him that wasn't going to happen tonight.

But she did want him. So he would follow her wherever she wanted to go. Once she made love with him again, maybe she would remember how much she loved him . . . and forgive him.

She slid open the patio door and walked across the grass. Her nightgown slipped from her body and wisped to the ground. Wearing only skimpy panties, she continued toward the pool. She stood on the side and dove into the water. A moment later, she surfaced and clung to the side of the pool with one hand. She curled in the water, and a second later she lifted her dripping panties from the water and tossed them onto the stone deck, then she smiled at him.

Oh, God, he wanted her. His heart ached for her. His body ached for her.

Still wearing his pajama pants, he dove into the water and swam toward her. He grabbed the side of the pool and flicked his head to toss his wet hair from his face. She gazed at him as he faced her, a sweet smile on her lips.

Her fingers entwined in his hair and she drew his face to hers, then pressed her lips to his. He dragged the tip of his tongue across her lips and glided into her mouth. She sucked, pulling his tongue deeper. Heat filled his groin. Her hands stroked down his sides, then around behind him to stroke his buttocks. He clenched, loving the feel of her delicate hands cupping him. Then her fingers curled under his pajama pants and glided over his naked skin as her thumbs pushed his pants downward. She squeezed his butt, then nipped his lips and glided down farther, pushing his pants down more.

He kicked them away as he stroked her hair with one hand. Her warm hands wrapped around his growing cock, then she grinned at him and disappeared under the water, descending his body as if climbing down a tree, then she hooked her legs around his calves to anchor herself. A second later, he felt her warm lips caress the tip of his hard cock, then she opened and took him into the warmth of her mouth.

He stroked her hair, almost gasping at the tender, erotic treatment of her mouth. She dragged her tongue over the tip of him, then squeezed him inside her mouth. When she began to suck, he did gasp.

Then her mouth slipped away and she surged to the surface to suck in air.

She grinned. "Maybe you should sit on the side for me, so I don't drown."

He chuckled and kissed her. "Whatever you want, sweetheart."

He grabbed the side of the pool and hiked himself up, then sat in the corner. His erection bobbed up and down. He could hardly wait for her to touch him again.

She propped her elbows on his thighs and wrapped her hands around him. She stroked, then grinned and swallowed his cockhead. She squeezed and sucked a few times, then released him and licked down his shaft. She lowered into the water and turned her head. From her position beneath him, she licked his balls. A moment later, she drew one of the soft, shaven sacs into her mouth. He groaned as she sucked on him gently, her hand lightly massaging the other sac.

"Oh, God, Crystal. I love that."

She released him from her mouth. "I know."

She shifted and pushed herself upward again, then nibbled his shaft with her lips, traveling to the tip again. She swallowed him inside, then glided up and down.

He couldn't believe he was here like this with Crystal again. After the despair of believing he'd lost her forever, this was sheer heaven. She touched him with such loving tenderness. Such concern for his pleasure.

She dove down deep, sending heat flooding through him. His balls tightened, and he knew he couldn't last.

"Honey, I'm going to . . ." He slid his hand along the crown of her head as she moved. "Oh, damn, that's . . ."

He sucked in air as she gazed up at him, nodding, his cock protruding from her mouth as she glided away. Then she surged forward again. He clutched her head and twitched forward, succumbing to the sensational heat of her mouth around him, squeezing him. He exploded, filling her mouth, the heat of his semen surrounding his cock. Then she swallowed and drew away.

"Sweetheart, that was mind-blowing." He leaned down and kissed the top of her head.

She grinned. "Well, I certainly was blowing."

She offered her hand, and he took it and pulled her from the water. He stood up and drew her to the grass, then sat down. She pressed him onto his back and prowled over him, then sat on his stomach as if holding him captive. He laughed and tugged her to his body, claiming her mouth. Then he rolled her over, trapping her between his hands.

"Now I think it's your turn."

"You think?" Her blue eyes glittered in the light of the full moon.

He chuckled again, then nuzzled the base of her neck and watched the goose bumps trail along her skin.

He kissed along her shoulder, then down her chest. When he reached her lovely breast, he kissed up the mound of softness, then licked the hard nub at the summit. She wrapped her hands around his upper arms and pulled him closer. He obeyed and drew her nipple into his mouth and sucked. Her sweet moan echoed through him. He licked, then sucked again.

She arched her pelvis upward. He kissed to her other nipple while his hand stroked down her rib cage to her stomach. She arched again, and he slid to the soft folds between her thighs. His fingers found the slick opening and he glided inside her.

"God, you're wet."

"Well, I was"—she sucked in air as he pushed in deeper and stroked her tight passage—"in the pool."

"Yeah." He nipped her nub again. "I don't think that's the reason." He grinned at her. "But maybe I should take a closer look."

He kissed down her torso and stopped at her navel.

"Have I ever told you how adorable this is?" He pushed his tongue into the cute little indentation.

"Yes, many times."

He could hear the smile in her voice. He kissed downward, loving the feel of her skin beneath his lips. God, it was as if she were made of warm, soft silk. When he reached her clean-shaven pussy, he paused, staring in awe. His fingers were still inside her, enclosed in the moist warmth of her, but it thrilled him to be this close to her lovely pink folds. He drew his fingers from inside her and pressed her thighs apart. To see her glistening opening up close. To be able to reach forward, as he did now, and run his tongue along her.

His heart soared. Soon he would hear the delightful soft sounds she made as he brought her to bliss. He would taste her honey sweetness as she erupted in orgasm.

He parted her folds with his thumbs and gazed at her slickness.

She shifted a little. "Hey, what are you doing down there?"

"I'm admiring you."

"That's not my best angle."

"Are you kidding?" He chuckled. "Anyway, is there somewhere you'd rather I be looking right now?"

"Well . . . no."

"Good."

At that, he stroked his finger along her opening, then licked again. She sighed. He glided his thumbs forward and opened to peer at the little button swelling inside the petals of moist flesh. He ran his fingertip over it, and she gasped.

---

Crystal threw back her head as she sucked in air. Brent's finger stroked her sensitive nub, then his tongue flicked against it. She murmured deep in her throat. Then he sucked. She forked her fingers through his hair and clung to him. He flicked her clit again and drew his head back, peering at her in the moonlight. She arched upward.

It had been wonderful touching him again, especially after believing she'd lost him forever. Feeling his hard cock in her hands and mouth . . . knowing she turned him on so thoroughly . . . sent her over the moon.

Now, with him touching her, his tongue driving her wild . . . she was in heaven.

His fingers glided inside her slick passage as his lips nibbled her tender flesh. He licked, then sucked again. Heat swelled through her and pleasure skittered along her nerve endings.

"Oh, God, sweetheart, you taste so good."

His fingers stroked faster and she arched again, then heat blasted through her. He sucked on her clit and she moaned as her whole body seemed to vibrate with intense energy. She gasped as blissful waves shuddered through her. She sucked in air and moaned again, clutching his head to her as an intense orgasm flung her to paradise.

Brent flopped down beside her. He took her hand and they lay there, staring up at the starry sky.


Evan watched out the window at Crystal lying flat on the grass, totally naked, Brent stretched out beside her. His heart ached. He hadn't meant to watch. Didn't want to see what he'd seen. But he'd been mesmerized. Hypnotized watching the woman he loved being drawn back to the man she should be with.

Guilt sidled through him at the thought that he never should have told her how he felt about her. Not only had it betrayed his best friend, Brent, but it had put Crystal in turmoil and caused the resulting pain of Brent leaving her at the altar. That wouldn't have happened if Brent hadn't seen Crystal kissing Evan.

If Evan hadn't told Crystal about his love, she wouldn't have suffered the pain of the last couple of days. She would be married to Brent now and they would be enjoying their honeymoon.

As he watched the two lovers stretched out on the grass under the stars, he realized that the universe had put everything right again. Brent had arrived to win back Crystal, and it appeared he had succeeded.

Evan's heart ached. But when he'd told Crystal how he felt, she'd kissed him with passion and . . . love. He was sure Crystal had feelings for him. He could tell by the way she looked at him. The tenderness in her eyes. The loving way she'd touched him. The passionate way she'd made love with him.

It wasn't his imagination. She had feelings for him. Sure Brent had found her first, but that didn't mean she might not love Evan more.

Except that there they were. Two lovers enjoying the delightful afterglow of their lovemaking.

He'd heard the splash earlier and had gazed out his

window to see Brent surfacing from a dive, then swim to Crystal. He'd watched, his heart sinking, unable to look away as they'd given each other pleasure.

They hadn't actually made love yet, with a full-out joining of their bodies. He was tempted to fly out there, to seduce her away or offer to get involved. Anything to stop Brent from claiming her again. But he knew that didn't make any sense. It was just the urge of a desperate man.

He wanted Crystal to be his so bad, he couldn't just stand here and watch Brent steal her back. But . . . he really didn't have any choice.

As Crystal gazed at the stars, warmth still flowing through her body, Brent pushed himself up on an elbow. The moonlight glazed his handsome features as he leaned toward her and captured her lips. His tongue swirled into her mouth and she opened to him, pressing her tongue tight to his and undulating. She felt herself swept up in his arms and he carried her toward the house and inside, then down the hall.

She'd left the door to the master bedroom open and he stepped inside, then set her gently on the bed. He closed the door. She watched him approach in the dim light of the room. Big, muscular. Sexy.

Her breath caught as she flashed back to the first time he'd made love to her. He'd wanted to make their first time special, so he'd taken her to a romantic restaurant in a charming little inn where they'd watched the sun set over the ocean. The fading golden light had shimmered across the water as they'd enjoyed their dinner.

Afterward, instead of dessert at their table, he'd surprised her by taking her to the room she hadn't known he'd reserved, where he'd had strawberries and champagne waiting for them. But by then, she wasn't hungry for food. When she'd nibbled his ear and told him so, he'd swept her up and carried her to the bed. They'd tossed aside their clothes and he'd ravished her body with kisses. When he'd finally joined with her, his big, hard erection pushing into her, she'd nearly come on the spot.

Anticipation quivered through her as she watched him approach her now. She longed to feel him inside her again. To feel his arms around her as he made sweet, passionate love to her.

A twinge of guilt flickered through her as she thought about Evan lying in the room next to them. Right now, her body ached for Brent, but could she do this? Could she really just forget about Evan?

Brent knelt on the bed and scooped her into his arms again, kissing her with a heated passion that made her blood boil. Feeling his arms around her, his body settling next to hers . . . The chaotic confusion within her collided with the intense need for him. She trembled and Brent smiled down at her, clearly taking that as a sign that she wanted him.

And she did. Desperately.

Deep in her heart, she knew she loved him.

He drew away and gazed at her, his brown eyes gleaming in the moonlight. She quivered at what his eyes revealed. It was so clearly there. Love. Filling his heart and overflowing onto her with a warmth that threatened to bring her to tears.

This man truly loved her.

She wrapped her arms around his neck and drew him back to her, opening her mouth as their lips joined, gliding her tongue into the warmth of his mouth. This was where she belonged. In his arms. Joining with him in the most intimate way possible.

"Make love to me, Brent," she murmured.

# Nine

Brent's heart swelled at Crystal's words. Not just because of what she asked, but because of *how* she asked it. With passion and deep need.

She still loved him. He could see it in her glowing eyes, hear it in her husky voice, feel it in her trembling body.

She loved him.

"Oh, God, Crystal. I love you."

She stroked his cheek. "I know." She nipped his lips with hers, then captured his mouth and tugged him to her to deepen the kiss. "Now show me how much."

He wanted to touch her everywhere, to kiss and nibble every silky inch of her. But right now, with her tongue gliding into his mouth the way he wanted to glide into her, her raspy breathing telling him just how much she needed him, he couldn't wait.

He stroked down her stomach and slid between her legs, then stroked her folds. Hot. And wet.

He wrapped his hand around his steel-hard, aching cock and pressed it to her slick opening.

"Oh, yes." She opened her thighs, inviting him in.

Slowly he pressed forward, his face inches from hers, watching her expression as his cockhead pushed inside. Her eyes flickered closed, then opened again, heat simmering in their depths. He continued forward, his shaft pushing deeper, caressed by the soft velvet of her silky sheath. She sighed and squeezed him, sending his heartbeat racing.

Finally, his entire cock filled her. He stayed like that, watching her, reveling in the feeling of being in her hot, tight grip . . . then slowly he pulled back. Her hands stroked over his shoulders, then she grasped them as he pushed forward again.

"Is this what you wanted, baby?"

She gazed at him through half-open lids as his cock filled her to the base. "Oh, God, yes."

He smiled and nuzzled her neck, then he drew back again. She wrapped her legs around his thighs as he pushed deep again.

"Oh, God, Brent. Make me come."

He groaned. "Honey, I could almost come just hearing you say that."

He drew back and plunged faster this time, then back and forward again. She squeezed him, setting his insides ablaze. He thrust and thrust. She moaned and arched against him. He cupped her behind and pulled her tighter to him.

"Oh, God, yes. I'm so close."

Her breathy voice against his ear acted like a catalyst. He pumped into her again and again. He wanted to blow right now, but he held back. Priming her. Filling her again and again until . . .

She gasped, and her hands tightened on his shoulders.

"Oh, yes, I'm . . ." She let out a long moan. "I'm . . . coming."

At those delightful words, he erupted inside her. She moaned and arched against him as he experienced the most intense orgasm he'd ever had.

He thought he'd lost her, and now he had her back. Knowing that had fueled the fire of his desire. Knowing that Crystal still loved him. And now they could have their happily-ever-after.

Crystal gazed at Brent's handsome face lying on the pillow beside her in the dark room. His breathing was deep and even. His warm physical presence so close to her and his arm around her waist made her feel loved and protected.

She tucked her hand under her head. But so did being with Evan.

Evan was so much fun to be with. He loved playing board games with her, which he did to keep her company when Brent had to work long hours, which happened a couple of weeks every few months. And Evan ran with her every Sunday. Brent liked to go to the gym and work out, but he wasn't a runner. So Evan would pick her up every Sunday morning and they'd drive out to the track.

They would joke and chat while they did their laps, then they'd go to Winnie's Diner afterward for the world's best pancakes.

Evan was always there when she needed someone. Like when she wanted to talk about something that was bothering her. Or to go out shopping for a gift for Brent.

And he had been there when she'd needed him most. When Brent hadn't shown up for the wedding.

God, how had she gotten into this mess? She'd invited Evan on her honeymoon, and now she'd have to send him away. After all he'd done for her. Guilt washed through her . . . but was that all it was?

Evan had seen her through the devastation of being left at the altar. With his caring and protectiveness, he'd shown her how much he loved her and how he would always take care of her.

And he'd made her aware of the feelings she'd been denying for him all along. Because deep down inside, she knew she had real feelings for him. Feelings that went deeper than friendly affection or sexual attraction. Maybe it was just infatuation. Or maybe it was something more.

She bit her lip. Could she really be in love with two men?

She loved Brent. She'd always loved him. But did that mean she should just ignore her feelings for Evan?

Her insides ached. Damn, what a mess. What would she tell Evan in the morning? She wouldn't lie and tell him she hadn't slept with Brent. She could hope it wouldn't come up, but that was just wishful thinking. And no matter what, she had to figure out what to do. Brent would expect her to ask Evan to leave. Or he'd do it. No man wanted another man on his honeymoon.

But it wasn't really their honeymoon, since they weren't married.

Brent had walked away as soon as something went wrong. Her gut clenched as she remembered how easily her ex-husband, Gary, had walked away after two years of marriage. She never thought Brent would walk away like that, especially on their wedding day.

She needed a man who cared enough to put an effort into making things work. He seemed to be trying to do that now, but was it too little too late? What would happen the next time something went wrong? Would he walk away then, too?

She stroked the hair from his forehead. A quiver raced through her.

She loved Brent, but would he see their marriage through?

Crystal woke up to bright sunshine washing across her face. Brent's arm was tucked around her waist, holding her close to his hard, masculine body. Although it felt cozy snuggled against him like this, she felt an overwhelming need to put distance between them. She felt guilty about spending the night in Brent's arms with Evan in the next room. Evan had feelings for her. He'd come here because she'd invited him after Brent had abandoned her at the altar. He had reasonably assumed they would have time, just the two of them, to explore their newfound relationship.

Then Brent had shown up.

She slid sideways, slipping out from under Brent's arm. He shifted, then rolled onto his back, still asleep. She pushed herself out of bed and pulled on her robe, then opened the bedroom door. As she headed to the kitchen, she could smell fresh brewed coffee.

Oh, damn. That meant Evan was awake.

"Good morning."

She glanced across the kitchen to see Evan sitting at the round glass table.

"Oh, hi." Self-consciously, she tugged the sash of her robe a little tighter as she walked toward the coffeepot. She poured herself a mug of coffee and added sugar and cream, then she leaned against the counter and sipped, wildly searching her brain for something to say.

Evan stood up and walked toward her, his face grim.

"I guess it's time for me to go."

Oh, God, he knew. Well, of course, he would figure it out pretty quickly when he saw that Brent wasn't in the sunroom. Maybe he had even heard them last night. Her cheeks flushed as she realized maybe he'd even seen them. He could probably see the backyard out the window of the guest room.

Okay, so taking Brent out to the pool hadn't been the best idea. But it was as if she'd been obsessed, needing to make love to Brent there, just as she had Evan.

She wanted to tell Evan he shouldn't leave, but what sense did that make?

"Evan, I'm sorry. When I asked you to come here . . ."

She hesitated, unsure how to describe what her intent had been. Should she really tell him she'd wanted to explore their feelings for each other with that option now cut off so abruptly?

"It's okay, Crystal. When we came here, we both thought things were over between you and Brent. Now he's back and things have changed." He leaned back against the counter, his face drawn in tight lines. "I guess my coming here was a mistake."

She rested her hand on his arm. "No, not a mistake." She didn't want him to think that. Ever. "What we shared was very special. I'll never forget it."

He smiled grimly. "In fact, that's a problem, isn't it?"

She understood what he was saying. How could they all remain friends with this between them? Brent would never forget that she had slept with his best friend, no matter the circumstance. How could Brent continue his friendship with Evan? How could she?

He squeezed her hand, then moved away. He poured some of the steaming hot coffee into his cup and took a sip, then placed the mug on the counter. "As soon as Brent gets up, I can pack the rest of my stuff," Evan said. "Unless you'd rather I go right away."

Oh, God, the problem was, she didn't want him to go. And she had a sinking feeling that if he went through that door now, she'd never see him again.

She stared at him, unable to utter a word, her heart tearing in two.

He loved her. And as much as she loved Brent, she

knew she was falling in love with Evan, too. She didn't want him to walk out of her life altogether. Her heart ached at the thought she might never see him again.

Sure, she'd almost married Brent, but he'd walked away and . . . maybe he wasn't the right man for her. Maybe Evan was. If she let Evan leave now, she'd never know.

If she let him walk out now, she could be making the biggest mistake of her life.

"Crystal? Do I leave now or later?"

She shook her head and set down her coffee mug. "I don't want you to go at all."

She stepped toward him and caressed his raspy cheeks, then pushed up on her tiptoes and pressed her lips to his. He hesitated, and she feared he would draw away, but then he wrapped his arms around her and pulled her tight to his body. Although she had initiated the kiss, his mouth claimed hers with passion, his lips hard on hers. His tongue glided along the seam of her mouth, then pressed inside. She opened, welcoming him, her body sizzling with desire for this man.

At the sound of a clearing throat, Crystal dodged back from Evan. Oh, God, Brent stood in the doorway, staring at them. Guilt surged through her as she glanced at Brent, then away.

The ensuing silence grated on her nerves and sent the tension level in the room skyrocketing. God, she didn't know what to say.

Finally, after what seemed like forever, Brent broke the silence.

"You'll notice I'm not leaving." He folded his arms across his chest. "I intend to fight for you."

"No need," Evan said. "We were just saying good-bye."

Evan walked across the room and picked up his suitcase, which was sitting by the table.

"I'll go pack the rest of my stuff and be on my way."

Crystal glanced from one to the other, her stomach clenching. If she didn't say something . . . if Evan walked out that door . . .

Evan stepped through the kitchen doorway to the hall.

"Wait," she cried.

Evan stopped and turned around. Brent sent her a sharp glance.

"We can't let him go," she said.

Brent's eyebrow arched. "I have absolutely no problem letting him go."

At his wry tone, Crystal swallowed. How could she tell Brent she wanted Evan to stay? Of course he didn't want Evan hanging around. He saw him as competition.

And he *was* competition.

But she had to remember that it wasn't just Brent's happiness on the line here. It was hers, too. And Evan's. And it was important that she get this right. She shouldn't just fall back into her relationship with Brent because he wanted her to. Maybe she should want to, especially after a two-year relationship and her promise to marry him. But life wasn't as simple as that. Brent walking out on her opened her eyes to some things. One, that she had strong feelings for Evan. And two, that maybe Brent wasn't the rock she'd come to believe him to be.

"I know you want Evan to leave. That you want to spend the next two weeks alone with me. I know you want to talk about what happened so we can get past it and move forward with our relationship." She couldn't bring herself to mention marriage. There was too much uncertainty inside her.

At the sour expression on his face, she realized that he didn't want to talk about it at all.

*Right, he's a guy. What was I thinking?*

"But . . . I'm afraid that . . ." She hesitated. "If Evan goes back now . . ." She glanced from one to the other. "The way it'll be between us . . . the awkwardness. I'm sure we'll never see Evan again." She glanced at Brent. "You won't want him around. You'll resent him." She turned to Evan. "And Evan will be uncomfortable being around us." At the rigid stance of both men, she knew this wasn't going very well. "You two have been friends for too long."

She knew how much they meant to each other. How deep their friendship had been. She didn't want that to end. If there was any way she could salvage that . . .

"Crystal, you can't honestly expect us to continue our friendship as if nothing happened," Brent said.

"No, you're right. The real issue is that something did happen." She stood up straight and pushed back her shoulders. "Evan and I have slept together. And we've discovered we have strong feelings for each other." She stared Brent straight in the eye. "And I don't think I can just walk away from that."

"Are you saying you're choosing him over me?" The pain in Brent's eyes tore at her heart. "But last night I thought . . . I was sure you still loved me."

"I do still love you."

"Then why would I stay?" Evan asked.

"Because I think I'm falling in love with you, too."

# Ten

"So let me get this straight." Brent leaned back in his chair and stared at Crystal.

After her shocking statement, they'd decided they needed to regroup. Go outside and get some fresh air. Now they sat at the table on the patio overlooking the pool and the glittering turquoise ocean beyond.

"You want Evan to stay at the villa with us?" Brent continued.

"That's right."

"In the next room?"

She hesitated.

His eyebrows arched. "Are you saying I'm going to be in the next room?"

"Well . . . uh . . . no."

Damn, she hadn't thought this out. She wasn't sure exactly what she was suggesting. She just knew she needed time to figure things out. And if Evan left this island and went back home, she'd probably never get the chance.

"I assume Crystal doesn't want me to just be a houseguest on your honeymoon," Evan said. "Don't you want to explore your feelings for me? See where that might lead?"

"And how is that going to help us patch things up?" Brent demanded. "I take it you're suggesting you have sex with him. While I'm sitting in the next room."

"And I assume she'll still be having sex with you, too. With me in the next room," Evan said.

Brent's hard stare latched on to her. "What exactly are you suggesting, Crystal?"

"Oh, God, I don't know exactly. This is hard on me, too. I didn't ask to be put in this situation. If I could unwind the clock to last Saturday, I would. Then you and I would be married now." A quick glance at Evan and the devastated expression on his face sent her heart clenching. "Except that would be a lie. I guess that's not what I want at all. All things happen for a reason. I believe that. And this happened so I'd wake up and realize that the attraction I felt for Evan couldn't be ignored."

"The attraction you felt for Evan? How long has that been going on?" Brent demanded.

Her stomach fluttered and confusion skittered through her. God, she'd already hurt one marriage because she'd had feelings for another man. Was she destined to ruin her relationship with Brent in the same way?

"It's not like that," Crystal responded. "I was attracted to Evan the first time I met him, but I was already going out with you. And I knew I was falling in love with you. So I suppressed my feelings for Evan, assuming they were just an attraction to a handsome, sexy guy. But when I thought you'd left me . . . when I faced those feelings without you in the picture . . ." She sucked in a breath. "Brent, if I'm really in love with you . . . ready to commit to you for the rest of my life . . ."

Oh, God, could she really say this out loud? She drew in another breath. "Then why am I feeling this way for another man?"

"That's easy. Because you were confused . . . hurt . . ." Brent's jaw clenched. "Maybe you even wanted to hurt me back."

Her heart constricted. "No." She leaned forward and stroked his cheek. "I would never want to hurt you. I hate that this whole thing is hurting you. But . . ." She didn't want to say this, but she had to. "If I were to just go ahead and marry you now, I'd always wonder. Should I really be with Evan? Did I choose you just because I met you first? I think in the long run, I would hurt you far more if we wound up getting married, then divorcing later."

His lips compressed. "We're not even married and you're already talking about divorce. I thought you were all about seeing it through the rough patches."

"So the alternative is staying together despite the fact that I might be in love with someone else? Living a lie?"

He took her hand and drew her closer. "I don't believe we've been living a lie. You love me, I know you do."

The fierceness of his tone thrilled her. He believed in them, and she felt the heat sizzling between them.

"You have to give me time to be just as sure as you

are. But until then, I need to explore my feelings for Evan."

"So," Evan said, "you're saying at the end of this vacation, you're going to choose between us?"

Brent glared at Evan, then shifted his hard gaze back to her. "Is that true?"

Her stomach twisted at the pain she saw in his face. She drew in a deep breath, then nodded.

Crystal walked along the beach, her sandals dangling from her fingers. The warm white sand squished between her toes as she walked. She'd had to get away from the building tension between the two men.

Three days had gone by since Brent had arrived. Three shaky days. After their conversation that first day, she and Evan had gone scuba diving, as they'd planned before Brent had arrived, then they'd all had dinner together, which had involved a lot of uncomfortable silences. That night, things got really awkward as bedtime approached, until finally she'd told them the only fair thing to do would be for them to all sleep separately. She needed time to figure all this out.

"Hey there. Beautiful morning."

Crystal glanced up to see a tall, leggy blonde woman wearing a short red slinky bathing suit cover, sunglasses, and a broad-brimmed straw hat walking along the beach, heading for a set of four lounge chairs with umbrellas. Her long, wavy hair caressed her shoulders and glimmered in the bright sunlight.

"Hi," Crystal said.

"Which villa are you staying in?" the other woman asked.

"Um . . . it's behind that gate right back there." Crystal pointed behind her at the wooden gate she'd exited to access the beach.

All along the beach were wooden fences that stopped people wandering from the beach onto the villa property beyond and gave privacy to the individual yards and pools. Their pool was well hidden, but the patio that overlooked the private pool offered a view of the ocean beyond.

"That means we're neighbors. My name's Sarah."

Sarah held out her hand and Crystal shook it.

"I'm Crystal." She glanced around. "It's pretty quiet. I'm surprised. It's such a beautiful beach."

"Well, this stretch of beach is reserved for the villas along here, and there are only eight of them. Right now, I know that includes a honeymoon couple, a couple celebrating their thirtieth wedding anniversary, and six college students sharing one. We're not likely to see the honeymoon couple, the students will probably spend all their time at the bars, and I've seen the older couple taking early morning walks. Then there's me and my guy. And you. I don't know about the other three."

"Actually, I'm part of the honeymoon couple."

"Oh, sorry. I hope I didn't embarrass you with that comment."

"No. Don't worry about it."

"So . . . where's the other half?"

Crystal's lips tightened in a straight line. "Well, it's complicated."

She didn't know why she hadn't just said he was having a nap, or reading the morning paper, or anything that didn't sound out of the ordinary. Now this Sarah would probably ask her about it. And maybe that's exactly what she was hoping for. Maybe she needed someone to talk to.

"Complicated? That sounds interesting." Sarah dropped her beach bag onto the chair. "I'm going to sit and soak in some sun. Want to join me?"

Crystal walked to the chair beside Sarah and dropped her sandals beside it. "Yeah, sure."

Sarah pulled a large blue-and-red towel from her bag and spread it out on the lounge chair, then she untied her wrap. Crystal's eyes widened as Sarah opened her top, revealing full round naked breasts. Crystal had been expecting a bikini top.

As Sarah slipped off the top, her shimmering blonde hair cascaded over her shoulders and around her rosy nipples. She pushed it back out of the way. From the lack of a tan line, clearly this wasn't the first time she'd been sunbathing like this.

"This is a nude beach?" Crystal asked.

"No. Topless is okay, but keep your pants on." Sarah laughed. "At least, that's the official line. But if you want to go all the way, it only matters if someone complains, and then you'll just get a warning from the management."

"I see."

Sarah sat on the chair and stretched out her long legs. She pulled a bottle of sunscreen from her bag and squeezed some onto her palm, then began spreading it over her shoulders and arms. She squeezed out a little more, then started rubbing it over her breasts. Crystal sat down, trying to ignore the woman as she caressed her breasts. It just felt a little too . . . intimate for a public place. Private beach or no, it was shared by eight villas. Someone might happen by any minute.

"So, why don't you tell me what's complicated." Sarah leaned back in her chair, the brim of her hat covering her eyes but the sun washing over her mostly naked body.

"Well, it's a long story." Crystal felt very conspicuous sitting beside the perfectly composed but bare-breasted Sarah, almost as if she should take off her own clothes so she didn't look out of place.

Sarah's full lips turned up in a smile. "I don't mind long stories."

Crystal glanced at Sarah. Should she really tell this woman what was going on? It was all a little strange and confusing, and most people would think her crazy for inviting Evan on her honeymoon. What would Sarah think of it all?

Crystal had a feeling that Sarah was not at all conventional and that she wouldn't even be fazed, but that was just a hunch, based on the fact that the woman didn't mind sunbathing topless.

Sarah tipped her glasses forward and peered over the rims. "I know we've just met, but if you're worried about unloading on a stranger, think about this. Since I am a stranger, it really doesn't matter what I think. I'm probably way better than talking to a sister or a friend because

I'm totally unbiased. And if you don't live in Chicago, which is where I'm from, we'll probably never see each other again after this vacation. So feel free to tell me whatever you want." She pushed her glasses back in place.

Crystal nodded. That made sense.

"Okay." She drew in a deep breath. "Last Saturday was my wedding day, and . . . Well, Brent—the man I was supposed to marry . . . he left me at the altar." Even though that was less than a week ago, it already felt like a lifetime.

"Wow, I'm so sorry to hear that." She pulled off her sunglasses and sat up. "So you came on the trip alone? Well, good for you."

"No, not exactly."

Sarah arched a well-shaped eyebrow.

"You see, the reason Brent left was because he saw me kissing Evan, his best friend."

"Really? Now I see why things got complicated."

"Evan kissed me, but then I told him I was still going to marry Brent." Man, this wasn't coming out in a very coherent manner. "You see, Evan told me he loves me and I was strongly attracted to him, but I ignored it because I love Brent. But when Evan told me that, I wound up kissing him. . . . Oh, God, I'm not explaining this at all well."

Sarah smiled. "Look, I get it. Evan sprang this on you right before the wedding. You kissed him because it just makes sense to kiss a man who'd just told you he loves you, especially one you have the hots for, but you came to your senses and told him you were still going to marry your fiancé."

"How did you figure that out?"

"Because you said he left you at the altar, not the other way around."

Crystal nodded. "That's right. But Brent saw us, only we didn't know. That's why he left. After that, my sister sent me off with Evan while she explained to the guests, and . . . well, Evan and I wound up . . . you know, being together."

"Sure, why not? As far as you knew, the groom had left you high and dry. This Evan is in love with you. You were on the rebound. I bet you're going to tell me next that you invited Evan on the trip with you."

Crystal nodded, thankful that Sarah was taking all this in stride, with no air of judgment.

"But that's not why it's complicated."

"Really?" Sarah said again.

"The day after Evan and I arrived here, Brent showed up wanting to win me back."

Sarah smiled broadly. "Oh, how romantic! So what happened then?"

"Well, Brent wanted to send Evan home."

"That makes sense."

"But I told him I didn't want to do that."

"Mmm. Now it's getting interesting. Do you still love your fiancé?"

"Yes, definitely."

"And how do you feel about Evan?"

Crystal gazed at her hands, lying in her lap. "I think I might be falling in love with him, too, which makes it even more complicated. I don't know how I'm going to explore my feelings for Evan while Brent is in the same house."

"Well, it seems to me you could simplify things quite a bit by simply suggesting a threesome."

Crystal's eyes widened. "A threesome? You mean me with both of them at the same time?" She shook her head. "Brent would never go for that."

"Would Evan?"

"I . . . don't know."

"And what about you?"

"Um. I've never really thought about it."

Which was an outright lie. Ever since she'd met Evan and felt the strong attraction for him, she'd fantasized about making love with him. Those fantasies had evolved into ones where Brent joined them and the two of them made sweet, passionate love to her. But that was a fantasy, not something she'd do in real life.

"Really? Never?" Sarah studied Crystal for a moment, then put her sunglasses back on. "So forget about what the guys might think. Does the idea appeal to you, now that you're thinking about it?"

# Eleven

Crystal's cheeks heated when she realized the idea of living out her fantasy appealed to her a lot. Both men, touching her, making love to her . . . That was hot!

"Yeah, I guess it does, but I couldn't suggest it to them. It's too . . . out there."

Sarah sent her a wicked smile. "You really need to loosen up."

Crystal sat up a little straighter. "I'm loose." Oh, that didn't sound right.

Sarah laughed, a soft, delicate sound. "Okay, then. Prove it." She pressed her fingertips to the tops of her breasts. "Join me."

"You mean, take off my top?"

"Sure. Why not? There's no one around. And even if someone does go by, what does it matter?"

Crystal shook her head. "I don't know."

"Come on. Why not? Be a little wild and crazy. You might like it."

Crystal pursed her lips. Maybe Sarah was right. She grabbed the hem of her loose T-shirt and pulled it over her head. Underneath, she wore her royal blue bikini. She reached around behind her and unfastened the hook. Then, with a quick glance around, she removed the top.

"There you go. Feels good, doesn't it?" Sarah stretched out on her chair again.

Crystal had to admit, it gave her a certain sense of freedom. And the sun shining warmly on her breasts felt wonderful. She leaned back against the chair and tucked her hands behind her head, reveling in her breasts being bared to the world.

Then she saw two men walking along the beach in the distance. Immediately, she wrapped her arms protectively over her chest.

Oh, God, what was she doing?

Sarah glanced in the same direction, then turned and winked at Crystal. "Don't sweat it. Just put on your sunglasses, lean back, and ignore them."

They were still a good distance away, but she suddenly realized that the two men were Brent and Evan. Probably out looking for her.

"Um, except . . ."

Sarah smiled. "That's them, isn't it? Your two men?"

"That's right."

"This is perfect."

"It is?"

"Yes. You like the idea of having a threesome, right, but you don't know how to convince them?"

"Um, yes, I guess."

"Okay, good." Sarah put her feet on the ground between their two chairs. "Sit up and face me."

Crystal did it, so they sat face-to-face.

"Wow, those two men are gorgeous." Sarah pulled the bottle of sunscreen from her bag again, then took Crystal's hand and squeezed some of the warm liquid in her palm. "Now rub it on my breasts."

"Uh, I don't think that's a good idea."

Sarah grabbed Crystal's hand and placed it over her breast. "Trust me. It's a fabulous idea."

Sarah guided Crystal's hand to move in a circle, then released it. Crystal kept her hand moving on Sarah's round, soft breast, unsure what else to do. If she just stopped, it would look as though she were fondling Sarah. The stroking at least didn't seem as bad. She shifted to the other breast, because that just made sense. Then she drew her hand away.

Sarah sighed, then squeezed some lotion into each of her own palms. A second later, Crystal suppressed a gasp as Sarah's hands encompassed her breasts. She stroked the warm lotion over and over her breasts. Crystal's nipples puckered and her insides quivered. Oh, man, she couldn't believe this was actually turning her on.

"Believe me, once the men watch this for a minute or two, you could suggest all four of us make out right here on the beach and they'd agree."

Brent drew in a breath as he realized one of the two topless women on the chairs ahead was Crystal. And the other woman was stroking Crystal's breasts. His cock hardened as his gaze glued to the woman's hands moving around and around over Crystal's lovely round breasts, the nipples puckering forward. A clear sign Crystal was turned on.

"My God, that's Crystal." Evan stopped in his tracks.

Brent stopped walking, too. They just stared at the two women in astonishment. The very attractive blonde had big, full breasts, and ordinarily he'd enjoy the sight, but right now he was mesmerized by her hands moving over Crystal's breasts.

God, he wanted to rush over there right now and help the blonde stroke those pert mounds. His cock ached with need, seeking escape from his boxers.

Crystal turned her head in their direction.

"Oh, hi. I've met a new friend."

"So we see." Brent started toward them again, and Evan followed suit.

The blonde kept rubbing Crystal's breasts.

"This is Sarah," Crystal said.

The blonde glanced in their direction and smiled. "Hi."

"Sarah is making sure I don't get burned."

Brent was sure that Crystal's breasts were thoroughly covered with lotion by now, but he wasn't going to complain about Sarah's continued attention on Crystal's breasts.

"I don't think you got mine fully covered," Sarah said as she finally drew her hands away.

She squeezed some lotion on Crystal's hands. After a brief hesitation, Crystal began rubbing Sarah's breasts. The sight of Crystal stroking the other woman that way made Brent's cock throb. Visions of Crystal kneeling in front of the other woman and stroking her nipples, then taking one into her mouth, flickered through his mind. He kept hoping that would turn into a reality.

Evan leaned in and murmured, "Is this turning you on as much as it is me?"

"Oh, yeah." His heart thundered in his chest as he watched Crystal's hands move round and round on the full breasts. His cock throbbed with urgent need.

Finally, Crystal released Sarah's breasts, almost reluctantly. Or maybe that was just his imagination.

Brent sucked in a breath. "Crystal, sweetheart, do you want to head back to the villa with us?" Damn, but he needed to get her back there. Quickly.

"You go ahead," Sarah said. "We can talk later. Drop by my place anytime." She reached into her bag and pulled out a small spiral notebook, then jotted something down. "Just poke your head in the back gate. If I'm not here on the beach, I'm usually by the pool." She ripped out the page and handed it to Crystal. "Here's my phone number at the villa, and the combination for the lock on the gate."

Crystal pushed the slip of paper into her own bag, then reached for her bikini top.

"Here, let me help you with that." Sarah tugged the top from her hand and pushed it into Crystal's bag.

Crystal grabbed her T-shirt and, with a hesitant glance toward Sarah, pushed it into her bag, too, then stood up.

"Nice meeting you, Sarah." Brent shook her hand, as did Evan.

"I'm in the villa next to yours. Hopefully, we'll see each other again."

He smiled and nodded, trying to concentrate on her words as thoughts of ravishing Crystal swirled through his mind. He turned to follow Crystal, then stepped to her side and walked with her. Evan fell into step on the other side.

Brent couldn't believe how much of a turn-on it was watching her walk along the beach almost naked, her soft breasts bouncing slightly as she walked. He slid his hand around her waist and pulled her close to him, needing to feel her body next to his. He wanted to stroke his hand over her round, naked breast, to feel the nipple tighten under his fingertips as he toyed with it.

God, as soon as he got her back to the villa he wanted to ravish her. But how could he do that with Evan there? Evan had to want the same thing.

They reached the gate and Evan opened it. Crystal stepped ahead as she climbed the stone steps up the incline, with Brent right behind her, as Evan closed the gate behind them. They passed the thick bushes and stepped into the well-manicured grounds behind their villa, the pool glittering in the sunlight.

"Oh, God, Crystal, I'm so turned on." Evan stepped past Brent and tugged Crystal into his arms and consumed her mouth.

Brent knew he should be annoyed or jealous, but the sight of her naked breasts crushed against Evan's hard, muscular chest, of their mouths moving passionately against each other, made his cock harden even more.

God, he needed to touch her. He stepped behind her and stroked his hands over her shoulders, then glided down her bare ribs. He slid his hand between their bodies and cupped her breasts. His cock lurched at the exciting sensations, not just of the feel of her breasts in his hand, but of Evan's hard flesh pressed against the backs of his hands and the heat of their two bodies pressing against him. His fingers found her nipples and he stroked the hard buds. She arched forward, pushing her breasts tighter into his hands. At the same time, she pushed her ass back into his crotch. She had to be able to feel his hard erection straining against his pants.

He leaned in and nuzzled her neck. "Crystal, I want to make love to you," he murmured against her ear.

Evan released her lips. "So do I."

Crystal turned between them, an impish gleam in her eyes, and stroked Brent's shoulders. "So both my handsome men want to make love to me. That is so hot."

Heat blazed through Brent and he pulled her against him, capturing her mouth with his. The feel of her naked breasts crushed against his chest sent his heart racing. And knowing Evan was pressed tight behind her, feeling Evan's hands slide between their bodies and stroke under her breasts, escalated his excitement. His cock ached as it pressed against her warm stomach. He pushed his tongue between her lips and tasted her sweetness. She melted against him with a soft sigh.

Crystal reveled in the feel of the two hot, hard bodies tight against her. She couldn't believe this was really happening. Evan's hands left her breasts and slid down her body. He brushed by Brent's hard bulge pressing against her stomach.

Brent sucked in a breath, his lips parting from hers, then stepped back.

She ran her hands along her arms, then over her aching breasts. "This is so sexy. I'd really love to feel both of you stroking me." She ran her fingertips over the distended nipples, sending heat thrumming through her. Both men stared at her fingers. She ran one hand down her stomach, then her fingers dipped under the elastic of her bikini bottoms. "All over."

Blatant lust shone in Brent's eyes, but his expression tightened. She could tell he wanted to do this but was holding back. He couldn't hide the effect on his body, though. She had felt his hard cock against her, and now a huge bulge strained at his pants. Evan's, too.

She pushed her fingers deeper into her bottoms and stroked her wet opening, hoping a little encouragement was all they needed.

"I'm so wet right now. I'd love to suck both your cocks."

She stepped toward them, allowing her gaze to drop to their crotches, her gaze shifting from one growing erection to the other. She drew her hand from her bottoms and stroked both men. Their cocks were so hard.

Brent wrapped his fingers around her wrist, stilling her hand. "Crystal, I don't know if I can do this."

Crystal saw the struggle in his face. She stroked his raspy cheek. "I don't want you to do anything you're not comfortable with, but it would be so hot. Is it really so bad to go a little wild and crazy?"

Evan stepped toward Brent and grasped his shoulder. "Man, this is something we've thought of doing for a long time. Sharing a woman."

They'd thought of doing a threesome before? Maybe this could happen. Maybe Brent just needed a little more encouragement. She glided her hands behind her neck, which thrust her naked breasts forward, and lifted her hair. "It would be so hot to be with both of you."

Evan's dark green eyes glittered with desire as he watched her. Brent's expression was unreadable, but he couldn't seem to tear his gaze from her.

She took Evan's hand and pressed it to her breast, her gaze locked on Brent. He watched, mesmerized. Encouraged, she unfastened Evan's jeans and drew down the zipper, then knelt in front of him and reached inside. She wrapped her hand around his thick, hard cock and drew it out. Smiling, she leaned forward and licked his tip. Evan groaned. She gazed up at Brent, her tongue still trailing over Evan's cockhead. Brent's eyes gleamed with need. She wrapped her lips around Evan's cockhead, swirling her tongue over him.

Brent watched Evan's cockhead disappear into Crystal's mouth. Rather than making him jealous, the sight turned him on immensely.

He and Evan had often joked about having a threesome with a woman. Something about the idea of sharing a woman with his best friend had been very appealing. As if it would strengthen the bond between them or enhance it in some way.

But this was Crystal.

Crystal gazed up at Brent, then reached over and stroked the bulge in his pants. His heart hammered in his chest. He flicked open the button of his jeans and pushed down the zipper. When her hand slid inside and wrapped around his throbbing cock, he thought he would come on the spot. Watching the two women caress each other's breasts, then Crystal walk back to the villa practically naked, had left him in urgent need. Now, with her hand around him, he didn't know how long he could hold it.

She drew his cock out of his pants while she continued to suck on Evan's cockhead. Then she released Evan's cock from her mouth and shifted a little closer to Brent. He groaned as her hot mouth surrounded his cockhead. Her tongue glided over his sensitive flesh in circles. The fact that Evan was watching turned him on even more. Then her mouth moved away and she swallowed Evan again.

His cock ached with need until her mouth returned again. When she sucked, it swelled even more, threatening to explode in her mouth. Slowly she took him deeper, squeezing him inside, then the tip of her tongue toyed with the ridge under his cockhead, gliding around in one direction, then the other. His hand raked through her hair as he concentrated on restraining his urge to let go.

She slipped from his grasp as she returned to Evan, who had watched her mouth on Brent's cock with intense concentration. She took Evan's cock in her mouth, then slowly moved down. She glided back, then took him deep again. His hand grasped her head and his expression tightened. She bobbed up and down, and Evan groaned, then shuddered, clearly coming in her mouth.

Brent's cock twitched as he watched, needing to feel her heat around him once again. She kept sucking Evan until he relaxed, having finished his orgasm.

She drew her mouth from his wilted cock, then turned to Brent again, her hand tightening around him. Before she could wrap her sensuous mouth around him again, he grasped her arms and drew her to her feet.

"I want to make love to you right now," he insisted.

He captured her lips, knowing Evan had just come in her mouth. Tasting Evan's seed in her mouth drove his need higher. He stroked her breast, then down her belly to her bikini bottoms. He slid underneath and cupped her mound, then slid his fingers along her amazingly wet opening. It seemed sucking Evan to completion had turned her on immensely.

"You're so wet," he murmured. "I'm sure you want my hard cock inside you right now."

He slid two fingers deep inside her and stroked her clit with his thumb.

She squeezed his throbbing cock. "Oh, God, I do."

He eased her to the ground, then kicked away his jeans and boxers. He knelt beside her on the grass and stripped off her bottoms.

"Damn, you look sexy lying there naked like that."

She wrapped her hand around his cock again. "Now, Brent." She opened her thighs. "Fuck me. Deep and hard. While Evan watches."

# Twelve

The thought of Evan watching them intensified his need. He desperately wanted to drive his aching cock into her right now. He positioned himself between her thighs and stroked her slit, loving her tiny whimpers of desire.

"Do you want me, baby?" he asked.

She nodded. He wrapped his hand around his cock and guided it to her and nudged against her slick opening.

"Tell me. I want to hear you say it."

She grasped his shoulders. "I want you, Brent. I want your long, hard cock inside me."

At her words, need lanced through him. He drove forward, filling her with one long thrust. She moaned, then held him tight to her body.

"You like that, sweetheart?"

"Yes," she whimpered.

He was aware of Evan watching them. His cock twitched.

"More," she pleaded. "Fuck me."

He drew back slowly, allowing his cock to stroke her tight passage. Her eyes glazed and she threw her head back with a moan. Slowly, he glided forward again. She clung to him, murmuring soft sounds. He drew back again, but this time he thrust forward. Then back, then forward again. She gasped as he drove into her again and again. His head swam with the effort to keep from bursting inside her. He thrust several more times and she gasped, then moaned long and loud. Liquid heat surrounded his cock and he exploded with incredible force. Pleasure flooded his body like never before.

And still he thrust, until she finally collapsed on the grass, panting for breath.

He rolled away from her and she sighed. He stared at the clear blue sky above, feeling as though this could well be heaven.

Until he realized that Evan now knelt in front of Crystal. Brent watched as the other man's big cock slid inside her wet opening. Evan surged forward and Crystal immediately gasped. Evan rode her fast and hard, and within moments, she wailed her release again.

Brent couldn't drag his gaze from that hard cock driving into Crystal. Possessing her. It filled him with a need for . . . something, but he didn't know what.

God damn it. He didn't understand these feelings.

Brent sat up and watched as his best friend continued fucking Brent's woman. Frustration surged through him. It shouldn't be that hard to figure out. His best friend was fucking the woman Brent loved. What the hell did he think these feelings were?

As Crystal wailed in ecstasy, Brent pushed himself to his feet and strode away.

Crystal heard the deck door open and close.

"Don't worry about it," Evan said. "He just needs a little time."

She gazed up at Evan. His cock was still a firm presence within her.

"But what if he thinks . . . I don't know . . . that I'm a slut?"

"For having sex with us both at the same time?" He chuckled and kissed her lips. "I'm sure he doesn't think that."

She sucked in a deep breath. Evan was so great. And his cock seemed to be getting bigger inside her.

"So why are you okay with this?" she asked.

He grinned. "With having sex with you? Are you kidding?"

"At the same time as Brent," she clarified.

"Ah." He pivoted his pelvis forward, pushing his cock a little deeper into her. "Because I want to keep in the game. I'm number two, so I have to try harder."

And he was getting harder inside her.

"So you don't really want to do it?" She didn't want to push him . . . either of them . . . to do something they were uncomfortable with.

He pushed in a little deeper. "I didn't say that. I actually found it really hot watching you suck Brent's cock.

And right there in front of me. In fact"—he pushed in a little deeper—"Brent and I have often talked about sharing a woman. This was actually a fantasy come true."

She could barely concentrate on his words with his big cock pushing inside her like that.

"Evan, you've already come twice. I can't believe you—"

He pushed forward, driving deep into her again, and she gasped. "I might not come again, but that doesn't mean I won't get hard." He nuzzled her neck. "And that I can't make you come again."

Excitement quivered through her. "I see. So watching me with Brent's big cock in my mouth turned you on?"

"Oh, yeah. And earlier, when you were with that woman on the beach."

"You liked watching Sarah put suntan lotion on my breasts."

"She wasn't putting suntan lotion on." His heated gaze simmered through her.

"She wasn't?" The feel of his cock slowly gliding into her again set her blood boiling.

"No. She was caressing you." He nibbled her earlobe, sending quivers down her neck. "Fondling you. Turning you on."

She grinned, happy to play along. "You're right. Her hands were so soft, and they felt so good on me."

"Tell me more." His cock glided away, stroking her inside passage, then slowly glided in again. "Did she touch your nipples?"

"Oh, yeah. As she was caressing me, my nipples got

really hard, then she stroked them with her fingertips."
She could feel his cock growing inside her.

"Really? Then what?"

"Then she leaned down and licked one."

He moaned and pushed deep into her. His hand
stroked over her breast and his fingers found her hard bud.
As he tweaked it, sending need thrumming through her,
she continued.

"She sucked it in her mouth. It got even harder."

"And your pussy?" His voice sounded hoarse, his
breathing labored. "Did she touch your pussy?"

The thought sent heat flaming to her cheeks, which
was ridiculous since she was lying out on the grass with a
man's cock inside her, after having made love with him
and another man only moments before. But the thought
of exposing herself totally on a public beach, of having
another woman touch her down there, made her uncomfortable. And yet, it turned her on immensely.

*God, it's just a fantasy. Enjoy it.*

"Yes."

He sucked in air and she could see the excitement on
his face. "Tell me."

"Before you got there, she pushed me back on the
lounge chair and stripped off my bikini bottom."

"Yeah?" His cock glided away, then pushed deep again.
Electric tremors quivered through her.

"She sat on the end of the chair and leaned forward,
then stroked me."

He sucked in air. "Were you wet?"

"Oh, yeah. Really wet."

His cock pushed deep, then back, and deep again.

"Then she leaned forward and licked—"

His cock drove deep and he groaned as he exploded inside her. So much for not coming again.

He kept thrusting into her, and she surrendered to the pleasure swirling through her. His cock filled her again and again until she gasped, blissful sensations erupting through her and catapulting her to another orgasm.

Brent stared out the window as Evan made love to Crystal again. God damn it. How had he wound up in this mess? He wanted his woman back. And he didn't want to share her.

And yet, watching her gasping in pleasure in the arms of his best friend sent his cock swelling to a rock-hard state. He longed to drive his cock into her at the same time as Evan, knowing Evan's cock was buried deep inside her. The thought of both their cocks gliding inside her, stroking close to each other, just a thin layer of flesh separating them, triggered a yearning deep inside him.

And that confused him.

Evan pulled Crystal to her feet, and the two of them headed toward the door. The sight of Crystal's naked breasts softly bouncing as she walked, her face and chest still flushed, sent his hormones spiraling out of control.

God, he wanted her right now.

The door opened and the two of them stepped inside.

"Oh, Brent." Crystal paused, gazing at him with big eyes.

He grabbed her arm and pulled her to him, capturing her mouth with his, his tongue storming inside, then plundering. He needed her to know that *he* was her man. He grabbed her wrists and backed her against the wall, pinning her hands over her head, then he kissed down her neck and found her nipple. The sweet bud tightened to a hard bead in his mouth, the surrounding skin puckering. He lapped his tongue over it again and again, loving her response to him. He released it and captured the other one, then sucked until she gasped.

"You're my woman and I want you." He half expected her to protest.

"Oh, God, Brent. I've never seen you like this."

He gazed down at her gleaming eyes and saw the heat there. She liked this.

Excitement lurched through him. "I want you now, and I'm going to take you."

She pushed against the grip of his hands around her wrists, but he held tight, then he sucked on her other nipple.

"No," she moaned.

His gaze flew to her face and he stared at her uncertainly. She stared back with simmering desire. His cock—pressed against her belly, compressed between the warmth of their two bodies—swelled even more.

"You can't just fuck me like this." But she nodded her head, obviously encouraging him.

He shifted his pelvis back and his heavy cock dropped

downward, then the tip nuzzled against her warm, wet opening.

Ah, man, he could barely stop himself from lancing into her like a barbarian.

*Easy, man.*

He eased forward, pressing into her slowly, feeling her hot, wet passage envelop him. His cockhead filled her, and she moaned.

"Oh, God, Brent."

In blind response to her desire-filled words, he thrust deep into her and she gasped. Then he began to move in and out like a piston, filling her again and again. He could feel her tighten around him, then gasp. He watched her face blossom in orgasm, joy washing across her features.

Oh, God, he loved this woman.

He released her wrists and glided his hand to her lower back, then pulled her tight to his pelvis as he eased her to the floor. He laid her back on the carpet, then stroked her hair as he continued to thrust into her, in slow and easy strokes this time.

Crystal, still floating on a cloud of pleasure, gazed up at Brent. His ferocious male energy just moments before had been wild and sexy. Now his tenderness touched her deeply. His cock filled her, and the pleasure still washing through her built into another wave. He moved faster, his warm brown eyes so tender and loving. His pelvis tightened, and as he erupted inside her, she gasped at another swell of pleasure. He pulsed inside her a few more times, and the swell launched to a tsunami, blasting her into yet another orgasm.

He collapsed on her, but still holding the bulk of his weight on his hands, which were flattened on either side of her. She stroked her hand through his hair, loving the feel of the dark brown strands as they curled around her fingers.

He smiled and kissed her. With the sweetness of that kiss, she had no doubt that he loved her.

But so did Evan, she reminded herself.

And sharing both of them had been incredible beyond words.

"I can't believe it. I've never had so many orgasms."

"Sharing two men will do that," Evan said from somewhere beside them.

Brent stiffened, and she realized he must have forgotten that Evan was still there watching them.

As incredible as it was sharing these two men, it was going to be a huge challenge.

Brent could hear the music as he walked alongside Crystal and Evan toward the welcome party for resort members. They were staying in one of the luxury villas owned by the same resort company that managed the huge complex of holiday condos farther along the beach.

The large resort pool where the party was being held was only a fifteen-minute walk from their place, so they'd elected to leave the rental car behind and enjoy a nice walk in the late afternoon sunshine.

They followed a stone path surrounded by gardens of tropical flowers and varied decorative foliage. Several three-story buildings were nestled among large bushes and palm trees. There were probably hundreds of units on the grounds, but the way the resort was laid out, especially with the generous use of greenery, each building seemed private and welcoming.

They'd all decided it would be good for them to get out together, the three of them. Interacting in a social setting would provide a welcome distraction from the tension of the past few days.

Beside them, Evan stopped and checked the paper where he'd scrawled the directions.

"It looks like we turn right here, then . . ." He glanced past the flowering bushes that parted to the right. "It must be through that gate over there."

Evan walked ahead, then slid his key card into the slot on the black wrought-iron gate and opened it. They walked through the gateway, then past the high bushes alongside a building to their right to a view of a huge pool with curved, meandering edges. Lounge chairs, most of them occupied by swimsuit-clad bodies or towels and beach bags, lined the white concrete deck surrounding the pool. People milled around the open area behind the chairs, holding tropical drinks and munching on snacks from trays offered by waitresses, each with a large blossom in her hair and wearing a bikini top and sarong. A waitress passed them and offered a tray of tidbits. Crystal took a square with a shrimp on top. Brent took a small meatball spiked with a toothpick. He nipped the meat from the wooden stick. Sweet and tangy. Not bad.

Another waitress passed with a tray of drinks. Crystal grabbed one of the stemmed glasses filled with dark pink liquid and took a sip.

"Mmm. Nice punch."

"I'm getting something stronger." Evan glanced toward Brent. "Beer?"

Brent nodded, then Evan headed off toward the bar.

"Brent, would you hold my drink?" Crystal smiled at him. "I'm going to the little girls' room."

"Sure." He took the stemmed glass and watched her walk away, admiring the sway of her delightful derriere.

She looked sensational this evening in her floral sundress. Halter style, leaving her tanned back totally bare. He loved that. What he loved even more was that she wasn't wearing a bra under it.

She disappeared from view. He swished the liquid in her glass and realized he was getting thirsty. A quick glance toward the bar, with Evan at the end of a long line, told him he'd have a bit of a wait. He gazed around the large pool area. Both other bars had similar lines, the large pool was filled with people, and more people kept entering through the gate. There seemed to be people everywhere.

Man, he was glad they were staying at one of the luxury villas. He hated crowds. He wouldn't be at this party right now if it weren't for the fact that he wanted to be with Crystal. He sighed and swirled her glass again. And, of course, he'd needed to get away from the closed-in feeling of the three of them together in that house. Sometimes three could feel like a crowd.

This evening would be good, though. Crystal liked parties and meeting new people.

He watched the people walking by, then glanced in the direction where Crystal had disappeared. She was walking toward him and smiled as she saw him looking at her. Then she turned, making a pointing gesture as she mouthed words to him. He couldn't tell what she was trying to say, but he could see she was heading toward an extravagant buffet table. She was probably checking out the food. Glancing toward the bar, he saw that Evan was now third in line.

When he looked back to Crystal, he saw a dark-haired man in a tropical shirt and shorts talking to her. She shook her head, then walked around the table to the other side. The guy followed her.

Damn it. He was hitting on Crystal! Anger surged through Brent and he strode through the crowd. As he approached, Crystal glanced his way and a big smile claimed her face. His heart melted, taking the edge off his anger.

"But I just want to buy you a drink," the guy said. "One little drink won't hurt."

"Crystal, here's your punch." Brent handed her the glass and glared at the other man.

"You're with him?" the guy asked Crystal.

"That's right. She's my fiancée," Brent proclaimed.

"Really?" The guy gazed at her hand. "I didn't see a ring on her finger."

# Thirteen

Brent's gaze darted to Crystal's left hand. Her ring finger was bare—she wasn't wearing the beautiful marquise-cut solitaire diamond ring they'd chosen together. It felt like a sharp punch in the gut.

Damn, she'd probably taken it off on their wedding day, after he hadn't shown. How could he not have noticed before now? Of course, an engagement ring had been the least of his worries over the past few days. But now it felt as though their connection had been severed.

His heart clenched. God damn it, whatever it took, he had to win her back.


Crystal saw Brent's stricken look when he noticed her naked ring finger. Damn, she didn't even know where the ring was now. If Evan hadn't retrieved it from the floor, hopefully Renee had found it when she came to finish packing up for them.

Crystal tucked her arm around Brent's elbow and the other man wandered away. Evan approached with two tall glasses of beer and handed one to Brent.

"Problem?" Evan asked, his gaze following the man walking away.

"Nothing I couldn't handle," Brent mumbled.

Evan said nothing, ignoring Brent's defensiveness. "So how's the buffet look?" he asked.

"Great." Crystal moved to the big stack of plates on one end of the buffet table and picked one up. She hoped things would improve as the evening wore on. Maybe being out with other people, with music and drinks to relax them, they could get into a party mood and forget about the tension between them.

They filled their plates with chicken and salad and tropical fruits. Evan found an empty table, and they sat and ate in silence.

"I wonder if Sarah and her boyfriend will be here," Crystal said. She would love the couple to join them right now and break the tension.

A couple approached their table.

"Do you mind if we join you?" the woman asked.

They were at a table with six chairs, and all the tables around them were taken. Crystal considered telling the woman the empty chairs were reserved for friends, but she didn't even know if Sarah would be here.

What the heck . . . meeting new people was part of the fun of a party.

The couple sat and they all introduced themselves. Soon another couple joined them and pulled up another chair, and they all chatted about where they were from and what they'd seen of the island so far. All Crystal shared was that they'd been enjoying the lovely private beach and sitting by the pool. The other two couples were, interested to learn that she was staying in a villa and had won it in a contest. No one raised an eyebrow at the fact that she was sharing it with two men, but then, why would they? They wouldn't just assume she was having sex with both of them. Or maybe they did and just didn't care.

The conversation drifted to sports, and the other women seemed as interested in the subject as the men. Brent and Evan chatted enthusiastically, and Crystal was glad they had started to enjoy themselves. She didn't know anything about sports, so she just let the conversation drift around her while she continued to eat, keeping a watchful eye out for Sarah. These new people were nice enough, but she felt no connection with them the way she had with Sarah.

As the sun set, dramatic colors streaked across the sky. As it became dark, glittering strings of lights coiled around the palm trees turned on, enhancing the festive mood of the party. Couples began to dance to the lively music. The woman sitting next to Crystal glanced at her date and nudged her head toward the dancers, and he obligingly took her hand and led her to the dance area by the band. The other couple soon followed suit.

"Crystal, do you want to dance?" Brent asked.

Crystal glanced uncertainly at Evan.

"I'll go get you some more punch," he said.

She smiled and followed Brent to the dance area. His hand curled around her back and he drew her close to his body. He was warm and hard-muscled, and she loved being this close to him.

"Brent, I'm sorry this has worked out the way it has. I know it's hard on you." She glanced up at him. "And I'm sorry if this afternoon made you uncomfortable."

He nodded but didn't say anything. She felt guilty and awkward, not knowing what else to say.

They continued to dance, but Brent said nothing more. He seemed almost . . . preoccupied. He did draw her closer to his body, though, and held her as though he never wanted to let her go.

She really hoped that after she made her choice, the three of them could find a way to continue their friendship. Brent and Evan had been as close as brothers for years. They relied on each other. They cared about each other. She would hate to see their relationship end.


Evan returned to the table with Crystal's punch, then sat and watched her dancing with Brent. This afternoon had been a strange and exciting turn of events. He and Brent had often talked about sharing a woman, though they'd kept it at a level that seemed more like kidding around, even though Evan was sure Brent found the idea as much a turn-on as he did. If Brent hadn't started dating Crystal, it might actually have happened, but Evan would never have suggested they do so with Crystal. Though if Brent had ever suggested it, he would have jumped at the chance.

Now it was actually happening.

He'd found it exciting to watch her be so uninhibited. She'd become wild and sexy. Watching her sweet
mouth wrap around Brent's cock, knowing Evan was
watching, was a major turn-on. Then watching Brent's
cock glide into her . . . God, Evan's cock was swelling
now just thinking about it.

But seeing her in Brent's arms now, snuggling close
to him while they danced, seemed more intimate than
what the three of them had done this afternoon. In each
other's arms like that, they seemed to share an intimacy
that made him feel like an outsider.

He wanted to hold her close like that. To be the
man she loved. Wholeheartedly and forever. Out on the
dance floor, it was just the two of them, in their own
world.

Ever since Brent and Crystal had become engaged,
Evan had felt a growing anxiety. He and Brent had been
very close for a long time. Even when Crystal and Brent
had started dating, they had included Evan in a three-way
friendship. When they got engaged, however, Evan realized that their relationship would change forever.

At first, he just forced himself to come to terms with
the fact that Brent would be married and although that
would change things, they'd still be friends. Over time,
however, Evan began to realize he loved Crystal, too.
And now that it was all in the open, there was even a
chance he could wind up with Crystal as his wife. And he
hoped Brent would still be his friend.

But Brent had the edge, so Evan had to keep trying

to convince her *he* was the man she should marry. He grabbed his beer and took a gulp, then stood up, ready to stride over to Crystal and cut in.

Just then Crystal glanced around, grabbed Brent's hand, and led him back to the table.

"Evan, I just saw Sarah," she said. "We're going to go find her."

He handed her the glass of punch and followed behind her, sorry he'd missed his opportunity to hold her in his arms. To establish the kind of intimacy with her Brent had just enjoyed.

She sipped her punch as they wound their way through the crowd, heading to the other side of the large pool.

A flash of blonde hair caught Evan's eye. "Is that her over there?" he asked, pointing toward the woman he'd seen sitting by the pool.

"No, that's not her."

"I'm pretty sure I saw her go this way," Brent said, heading to the right toward an exit. "She was wearing bright blue, right?"

Crystal nodded, put down her glass on a serving table, then followed behind him. Evan trailed behind, jealous that Brent still held her hand. They went out the gate and wandered a little ways until they found themselves in a parking lot.

"Maybe they drove over here."

"You're sure it was her?" Evan asked.

"Yes, it was definitely her. And she was with her boyfriend—or I assume that's who he was—but we lost sight of them when we left the dance floor."

"I think if we walk over that way, we'll find the path back to the villas," Brent said.

"I guess," she said. "We wouldn't catch up with them now."

"Do you want to go back to the party and hope we spot them again?" Evan asked. "Maybe do some dancing?"

"Or call it a night?" Brent suggested.

Crystal sighed. "I guess we should just go now."

Although Evan was disappointed he couldn't hold her close on the dance floor, he was anxious to find out what she had in mind for sleeping arrangements tonight. Would she suggest all three of them share a bed? And if she did, how would Brent react?


Evan walked alongside Crystal as they strolled along the well-lit stone path lined with thick, well-trimmed bushes, Brent on her other side. The music and laughter from the party behind them merged with the sound of the ocean waves rolling along the beach.

Then he heard a noise. It sounded like a woman giggling.

"That sounds like Sarah." Crystal turned onto a side path.

It seemed to lead to a garden, lit only by the glow of the full moon.

Evan had a good guess what the couple was doing, but he was pretty sure Crystal had no idea.

"Shouldn't we just head home?" he asked. "They might want to be alone."

"Oh, I don't think they'll mind if—" Crystal stopped in her tracks.

Evan peered beyond the bush beside them and caught sight of Sarah and a man ahead.

Crystal ducked behind the bush again, but she couldn't seem to tear her gaze from them.

Sarah was crouched in front of the man, holding his cock in her hand. And it was the biggest cock, bar none, Evan had ever seen. Probably Crystal, too, judging from her widened eyes.

Sarah stroked the huge member, then pressed her lips to it. Evan could feel his groin tighten at the sight. She swallowed the huge cockhead in her mouth, then eased down the long shaft.

The sight was extremely erotic, but what turned Evan on even more was the sight of Crystal practically salivating. He was sure it was having the same effect on Brent, given the way he gazed at the couple, then back to Crystal, then at the couple again.

Crystal knew she should look away, but she couldn't. Sarah's boyfriend had the biggest cock she'd ever seen. It was huge, and she longed to be Sarah right now. Holding that big cock in her hand. Stroking it. Feeling it fill her mouth. Just as it did Sarah's right now.

God, what would it feel like to have that cock drive into her? To fill her. Stretching her. Gliding in and out of her.

Suddenly, she became aware that Brent and Evan were standing beside her.

"We . . . uh . . . shouldn't be watching this," she whispered.

"As long as we're discreet, it shouldn't be a problem," Evan responded quietly. "If they're doing this here, then part of the attraction is that someone might see them."

She tore her gaze from the man's huge erection to glance at Evan. "You think they want us to watch?"

"I'm not saying we should waltz out there and announce ourselves. I just mean that knowing someone might see them enhances their enjoyment."

Brent was extremely turned on. Watching the attractive Sarah crouched in front of the man, sucking his big cock, was arousing to say the least, but seeing how much it excited Crystal was an intense turn-on. He could see the outline of her hard nipples pushing against the soft fabric of her halter dress.

God, he wanted to get her home and fuck her silly. But would he have to share her with Evan?

At that thought, his cock tightened even more, which sent him into a spin. He didn't understand why he felt this way. He knew he wanted Crystal to himself, so why did the thought of sharing her with Evan seem to turn him on?

The memory of Crystal's uninhibited behavior this afternoon sent his hormones swirling. Evan had taken to the situation with ease, and that could only work in his favor, putting Brent at a disadvantage. As much as he hated the thought, he and his best friend were in competition for the same woman.

Evan's words triggered an idea. Why not show Crystal he could be a little wild and crazy, too?

He clamped his hand around her shoulder and tugged her into his arms for an explosive kiss.

"I think watching this has gotten us all a little hot," he murmured against her lips, then captured them again. "It's given me an idea."

He took her hand and tugged her back to the path, then hurried along it. Evan followed them.

"Where are we going?" Crystal asked as they raced along.

"To the beach."

The private beach behind their villa would be perfect.

Ten minutes later, they reached the gate. Brent pushed his key card into the slot and the latch on the wrought-iron gate gave way with a click. He pushed it open, then towed Crystal across the sand until they'd put a little distance between them and the gate. Then he turned and tugged her to him again, kissing her passionately. His hand traveled down her back, and he cupped her curvy ass, pulling her tight against his groin.

"Right here?" she murmured. "But . . . Sarah will be coming back this way soon. They'll see us."

"Over there." Evan pointed toward the rising cliff a little ways ahead.

Brent knew that the cliff face curved inland, providing

a sheltered space that wasn't visible from the rest of the beach. "Right. That's past Sarah's gate."

Crystal smiled, then curled her hand in his and started to run, towing him along behind her. Evan kept up with them easily.

# Fourteen

Once they were past the bend, Crystal stopped running and turned, smiling. This was a good sign. Brent had suggested coming here, and he hadn't tried to ditch Evan. Maybe he was warming up to the idea of the three of them, at least for now.

Evan grabbed her and tugged her into his arms, then captured her lips. The hard bulge in his pants pressed against her belly, just as Brent's had. Watching Sarah and her boyfriend had gotten them all a little horny.

Actually, a lot horny.

As Evan kissed her, Brent ran his hand over her behind, sending heat thrumming through her. Then he stepped closer, pressing his body against hers, his cock pushing against her ass. His hands glided along her thighs, pulling her skirt upward. He stroked over her bare buttock, then his fingers ran along the elastic waist of her thong.

Evan stroked her breast, sending pleasure careening

through her, then his hand glided inside her halter top and his warm palm cupped her bare breast. Brent drew her zipper down and unfastened the ties behind her neck. Her dress slipped away and pooled on the sand at her feet.

Evan glanced down at her naked breasts, caressed by the moonlight.

"Beautiful." His eyes glimmered with passion.

Brent, now shirtless, stepped beside Evan. "Hey, buddy. My turn."

Brent drew her to his body, then held her against him as he kissed her. At the feel of her naked breasts pressed against his hot, hard chest, tingles danced through her. Evan shed his shirt and pants and stood beside them in only his boxers.

She could feel Brent's bulge hard against her. She drew her lips from his and glanced at Evan. His erection pushed at his boxers. She wanted to feel those hard cocks in her hands. In her mouth.

She stepped back and gazed at them both, then glanced behind her. Several large clumps of rocks lined the cliff. She spotted one nearby that was the perfect height for sitting, and she headed for it.

"Follow me," she said.

"Anywhere," Evan answered.

She sat on the rock and stared at them expectantly.

"I want to see those beautiful cocks of yours," she said.

They both grinned, then pushed down their boxers, revealing their impressive erections. Evan's was thick, with purple veins curling along the shaft. It pointed straight up, while Brent's longer, more streamlined cock curved a bit to the right. The men stepped toward her.

She wrapped her hands around them and squeezed lightly, then stroked the hot, hard flesh. She leaned forward and licked Brent's tip, then Evan's. She urged the men closer and pressed their cocks together, then licked them both. God, it was so exciting feeling both their cocks under her tongue. Brent's body had tensed when their cocks touched, but when she kissed his shaft, then swallowed the cockhead into her mouth, he seemed to relax. She squeezed him and sucked, loving his deep murmurs of approval. His hand glided over her head, then stroked back her hair. She took him deeper, then moved up and down a few times, her lips gliding along his hard, hot flesh.

She released him and smiled, then licked Evan and took him in her mouth. She sucked him, then glided deep. After a couple of strokes, she released him. Both their cocks were so hard, she thought they'd burst.

Brent crouched in front of her and stroked along her inner thigh, sending goose bumps dancing across her skin. When he glided along her slit, the satin of her thong a thin barrier to his penetration, she moaned softly.

"Your panties are wet." Brent slid his fingers under the satin crotch and slipped inside her. He stroked her inside passage a couple of times, sending electric thrills humming through her, then he drew his fingers free.

He stood her up and glided her panties down, then stepped behind her. Evan cupped her breasts and stroked, then tweaked her hard nipples as Brent eased her legs apart. He leaned her forward and licked her wet slit. She gasped, then moaned as Brent found her clit and pressed against it with his tongue. Evan nuzzled her neck, then slid under her and took her nipple in his hot, wet mouth. He began to suck as Brent continued to lap at her clit. Pleasure rippled through her, sending her head spinning.

"Oh, God, I'm so close."

Brent pulled her to her shaking feet and then dropped back onto the ground, his awesome cock towering upward. She desperately wanted that monster inside her. She crouched over him and grabbed his big cock, then pressed it against her slick opening. She lowered herself slowly, his hard flesh stretching her as it glided inside. Behind her, Evan cupped her ass, then stroked round and round. Brent's cock pushed deeper into her.

Suddenly, she imagined it was Sarah's boyfriend below her, his big cock stretching her with its girth. She groaned and dropped down on him.

"Oh, God, fuck me right now," she pleaded.

Brent rolled her onto the soft sand. His cock pushed deeper as he gazed down at her with glittering eyes. Then he drew back and thrust forward, the ridge of his cockhead dragging along her sensitive inner flesh.

"Oh, yes."

His cock pushing deep into her nearly set her off. Heat burned through her, and she gasped as he plunged deep again.

She gripped his strong shoulders. "Fuck me hard."

"Whatever you say, baby." Brent drew back and lunged forward again, impaling her deeply.

The first wave washed through her, then swelled as he thrust again. Her whole body vibrated with sensation. His cock stroked her insides again and she wailed, flying into the abyss, her body quaking with bliss. Time floated like a cloud as her orgasm flared intensely.

Brent groaned, then erupted inside her. Finally he collapsed on her, then rolled to her side. She glanced at Evan, his cock still hard and bobbing in front of him. She opened her arms to him and he lurched forward, then prowled over her. His cock brushed her wet opening, then he thrust deep.

"Oh, yes."

He was so hard and thick. He thrust and her pleasure escalated again, then exploded through her like star-bursts. Evan groaned and she hugged him tight as ecstasy vaulted through her again.

Crystal stepped into the villa and headed straight for the bathroom. After shaking the sand out of her clothing and throwing it in the laundry basket, she took a shower, washing the sand from her body and her hair. When she returned to the living room, she found Evan sitting on the couch, an open bottle of wine and three glasses on the coffee table in front of him. From his damp hair, she realized he must have showered in the guest bathroom.

"Where's Brent?" she asked.

"He's taking a shower, too. We thought we might all watch a movie. You game?"

She sat beside him and took the glass of white wine he offered her. "Sure."

He walked to the cabinet beside the big-screen TV and read out the titles of the Blu-ray Disc movies in the extensive video library, and she chose a recent romantic comedy. When Brent returned, he sat on the other side of her on the couch and they relaxed.

While she watched the movie, she kept wondering what she'd do when it came time to go to bed. She took another sip of wine.

Crystal blinked her eyes open to bright sunlight. Her cheek rested against a hard, masculine chest. She glanced around and realized she'd fallen asleep on the couch, leaning against Evan. Brent's head rested on her lap. She shifted, feeling a little squished, and Brent's eyes opened.

"Morning," he murmured as he sat up.

"Good morning." She pushed herself upward, too. Her back was a little stiff.

"Did we all fall asleep during the movie?" Evan asked as he stood up and stretched.

"Well, you two did," Brent said. "I just found it so cozy snuggled against Crystal that I couldn't bring myself to leave."

And didn't want to leave her alone with Evan, no doubt.

"I'll go make some breakfast." Evan headed for the kitchen. "Western omelet okay with everyone?"

After they finished breakfast on the patio, enjoying the beautiful sunshine and the glittering ocean view, Crystal suggested they go to the beach. Once they arrived, however, and Crystal realized Sarah was sitting on the same chair as yesterday, she felt a bit self-conscious. The guys, however, seemed perfectly at ease.

"Mind if we join you?" Evan asked, his gaze gliding over her naked breasts, then settling on her face.

"Not at all." Sarah put down her book and smiled. Just like yesterday, this morning she wore only a bikini bottom, a big straw hat, and sunglasses. Her red bathing suit cover spilled out from the beach bag lying on the sand beside her chair.

Crystal sat on the chair beside her while Evan pulled a Frisbee from Crystal's bag and the two men raced across the sand toward the water. Crystal watched as Evan dropped the Frisbee onto the sand, then ran into the water, Brent right behind him.

You're quiet this morning. Is there something wrong?" Sarah asked.

"No." Except she couldn't get images of Sarah sucking that huge cock out of her mind.

Sarah leaned forward and gazed at Crystal's face. "Hmm. Either you've gotten a sunburn on your face, or you're blushing."

Crystal glanced at her, then dropped her gaze.

"What's on your mind, Crystal?"

Damn, maybe she should just tell her. Get it out in the open.

"Well, uh . . . it's just that, I was looking for you at the resort party last night and . . . well, we thought we saw you leave and we . . . um . . ."

"Oh, I get it. Did you happen to catch sight of Kade and me having a little fun on the way home?"

Crystal's gaze shot to Sarah's face. The other woman didn't even blush at the thought. Crystal remembered what Evan had said, about the idea that the possibility of being seen made it even more exciting.

"You don't mind?"

Sarah shrugged. "It's kind of fun knowing the three of you were watching us. Did it lead to anything on your side?"

"Um . . . well, it did give Brent an interesting idea."

"So did the three of you make out while you watched us?"

"Oh, no. Nothing like that. Brent just opened up a bit and . . . well, we made love on the beach."

"Really? That's great. Now when you say 'we' . . ."

"Uh, it was Brent and Evan and me."

Sarah laughed. "That's great, honey. So the three-some idea is working out okay."

"Yes. It was a little shaky at first. Brent wasn't comfortable with the idea, but after seeing you and Kade, he seemed to warm up to the idea."

"At first? You only started yesterday." Sarah grinned. "I assume you all did something after leaving the beach in the afternoon. The guys seemed really turned on."

"Yes."

"Good for you." She grabbed a bottle of water from

her bag and took a sip. "Having two cocks inside you . . . there's nothing like it."

Crystal shifted in her chair. She was sure Sarah wasn't talking about one of those cocks in her mouth.

"We . . . uh . . . haven't really done that."

Sarah's eyebrow arched. "Really? Why not?"

Crystal just shrugged, her cheeks burning. She wasn't sure what she thought of the whole idea of experiencing double penetration.

"Being sandwiched between two men, both of them pumping into you . . . that's hot!"

Crystal's cheeks flushed hotter.

Sarah quirked her head. "What have you been doing during your threesomes?"

"Well, they've really just been sharing me. You know, first one, then the other. I mean touching me at the same time, but . . . it's more like they're taking turns."

Sarah nodded. "I see." She leaned forward as if to share a confidence. "Have you ever had anal sex?"

"Um . . . yes, I have. With my ex-husband. But . . . I didn't really like it."

Sarah nodded again. "Is it possible he rushed it a little too much or . . ." She gazed at Crystal kindly. "Maybe you didn't totally trust him? I don't mean that he'd purposely hurt you, but . . . maybe you weren't as in sync as some lovers are. I mean, you are exes, after all."

"Are you saying that if I really trust Brent and Evan"—which Crystal knew she did—"that it would be different?"

"Definitely. At the very least, you'd be more relaxed.

If you know they want to please you, and you trust that they can read your signals, then you won't worry that they'll go too fast or push you past your comfort zone." Sarah rested her hand on Crystal's arm. "I know a lot of people have issues with anal sex, but it's really incredibly pleasurable." She watched Evan, his muscular form gleaming in the sun as he raced along the beach to catch the Frisbee Brent tossed to him. "I've sure been missing it lately."

Crystal glanced at her. "Why?" Immediately, she felt self-conscious at having asked the question.

An impish grin claimed Sarah's lips. "You saw Kade yesterday, right? Well, I am adventurous, but I'm not quite ready to take on that enormous piece of equipment."

"Oh." Crystal could think of nothing else to say. She had trouble imagining a modest-size erection gliding inside her there, let alone someone as enormous as Kade. Not that either Brent or Evan could be considered "modest." They both had deliciously generous penises, but Kade . . . his was in a whole different league.

Sarah took off her sunglasses and, leaning back in her chair, gazed at Brent and Evan. She nibbled on the arm of the glasses, watching them throw their Frisbee back and forth.

"You know, I have a suggestion that might help both of us."

At the intent interest in Sarah's eyes as she watched the men, Crystal's curiosity soared.

"And what's that?" she asked.

Sarah glanced in her direction and smiled. "Well, you

seem to want more excitement in your sexual experiences, as attested to by the fact that you enjoyed watching Kade and me last night. . . ."

"I didn't say I enjoyed—"

"It got you excited, right?"

Crystal couldn't deny it.

"So, given you like to watch, and given that I'd love to have anal sex, and DP even more, I was thinking that . . . maybe you could loan me your two men."

# Fifteen

Crystal's jaw dropped. She didn't know what she had expected, but it wasn't that.

"Just think about it for a minute," Sarah said. "You're all finding it awkward having a threesome. It would help all of you having someone experienced guide you, especially if you haven't done DP before. The guys could get practice with me, then you get the advantage. And you'd be there watching. That way it won't be like they're cheating on you, and you can see how exciting it can be."

"What about Kade? Won't he mind you being with other men?"

Sarah waved away Crystal's question. "Kade and I have a very casual relationship. We're more like close friends who sometimes have sex. Neither of us has been in a relationship for a while, so we decided to do this vacation together. He absolutely will not mind if I have sex with your two guys."

"This is crazy. Even if I agreed, they'd never agree."

Sarah laughed. "Are you kidding? They're guys. You'd be offering them the chance to have a threesome with no strings attached. And with your approval. Of course they'll agree." She smiled. "Especially if you say it's going to help you."

Crystal glanced at her two men. They'd dropped the Frisbee on the sand and were now walking waist-deep in the water, sun glistening on their damp hair and broad shoulders.

She had no doubt they both loved her and wanted to be with her more than any other woman, but she had to admit that if she made the offer to them—that they could be with Sarah without affecting their relationship with Crystal—they'd be interested. She wasn't sure if they'd actually follow through, but if she could convince them she was totally okay with it . . . they probably would.

Still, with all the emotional drama going on, now didn't seem like the best time to be experimenting like this.

"I think we need to get our situation worked out before adding another person to the mix," Crystal said. "The idea definitely sounds intriguing, but it's not good timing."

Sarah shrugged. "Suits me, but keep in mind—if you're trying to figure out which guy is truly compatible with you, then you shouldn't hide your true desires. Let your freak flag fly, as they say. The right man will come and join you."

Crystal nodded, but she wasn't so sure. Brent was definitely the more conservative of the two men, and even though he might not be as adventurous as Evan, that didn't mean she and Brent weren't a good match. On the other hand, would it be possible now that she had walked a little on the wild side that she would start to feel stifled by Brent? Sure, Brent had pushed into new territory when he'd dragged her off to make love on the beach with him and Evan, but she had a feeling his taste for adventure would be short-lived, ending with the end of this vacation.

"And just so you know, I would be totally amenable to you borrowing Kade," Sarah said. "I bet you're curious about what it would be like to ride that big cock of his."

"Oh, no, that's not necessary. I mean, I already have two men and—"

Sarah raised her hand. "Don't worry about it, honey. The offer's there if you want it."

Oh, great, now Crystal couldn't get the image of that big cock out of her mind. The thought of it sliding into her, stretching her, sent her blood boiling.

"So you'll think about it?" Sarah asked.

"Think about what?"

Crystal jumped at Brent's voice. Her attention on them had wavered, and she hadn't realized they'd been walking back.

Sarah smiled. "I just asked Crystal if I could borrow something, but I think she needs a little time to decide."

Brent glanced at Crystal. She shifted in her chair. Thankfully, he didn't ask what Sarah wanted to borrow.

"So what did she want to borrow?" Evan asked as he followed Crystal through the back gate, Brent right behind them.

Crystal hesitated.

"You don't have to loan her something if it makes you uncomfortable." Evan didn't like the look of panic in Crystal's eyes.

She glanced at him, then drew in a deep breath. "It does make me a little uncomfortable, but that's not a good reason not to do it."

"Why do I get the impression this isn't really about loaning her something?" Brent's eyebrow quirked up.

"It is. It's just that, what she wants me to loan her is . . ." She glanced at Brent, then Evan. "You."

"Me?" Evan asked.

"Actually, both of you. She said she'd love to have a threesome with the two of you."

"What the hell?" Brent's jaw dropped.

Evan's groin tightened at the thought of the beautiful blonde stripping off her bikini bottom and lying naked on the white sand, inviting him and Brent to ravish her.

"While I watch," Crystal continued.

His cock swelled at the thought of driving into the blonde while Crystal cheered him on.

"She was joking, though, right?" Evan asked. The woman couldn't be serious. Women didn't just discuss borrowing other women's men. On the other hand, a week ago he never would have thought Crystal would embrace a threesome with Brent and him, either.

"No, she's totally serious. And I'm wondering if"—she

shrugged—"I don't know, maybe it would help us all relax a bit about the situation we're in."

"The situation?" Evan asked, eyebrows raised.

"Yeah. The fact that I've had sex with both of you is making things weird between us. But"—she gazed at each of them—"sex is just sex, and if we can look at this whole thing as just an exciting and fun interlude we shared, maybe this won't have to hurt our friendship. No matter which of us winds up together . . . I'm hoping we can keep our friendship intact."

Evan did, too.

"What does us being with Sarah have to do with this?" Brent asked, his expression closed.

"Having a threesome with Sarah might put things into perspective. You can have a threesome with her, and since you don't have feelings for her, your emotions won't get in the way. Then later, when you think back on this vacation, no matter which of us winds up being a couple, we can all look back on this trip as a time of experimentation and sharing."

"I think you feel a little guilty about sleeping with more than one man," Evan said with a teasing grin, "and hope that sending us off to another woman will even things out."

She smiled. "Well, no matter what, if you decide to go for it, at least you two will have a little fun."

"It would be a nice distraction." Evan grinned at Brent. "What do you say, buddy? Sharing a woman? And since we don't have an emotional attachment to Sarah, we can just relax and enjoy it."

"Crystal, are you saying you'd be okay with this?" Brent asked.

She glanced at him thoughtfully. "I don't know. I think . . ." She shrugged. "Maybe I would be."

The next afternoon, Crystal opened the lock with the combination Sarah had given her, then stepped through the gate, conscious of Brent and Evan following close behind. They walked up some stone steps until they came to a path that led past some foliage and then opened up to a pool area. Sarah sat in a chair by a rectangular glass patio table, looking dazzling with her long waves of golden hair glittering in the sunlight, caressing her sun-kissed shoulders. She wore a turquoise bikini with a sheer floral sarong and an underwire top that pushed her full breasts up and out. The men's gazes locked on her as she turned and smiled, glowing like an angel.

Good God, beside Sarah, Crystal doubted the men would even notice she existed anymore.

"Hello." Sarah smiled. "I'm glad you could come. Please come and sit."

Crystal walked toward the table and sat down beside Sarah. Brent and Evan sat across from her.

"I've made piña coladas. Is that okay for everyone?" Sarah asked.

"Absolutely," Brent said.

"Fine with me," answered Evan.

Crystal simply nodded when Sarah glanced her way. Both men watched as Sarah walked toward the bar, where she had a pitcher of drinks all ready. She poured the frothy white liquid, then returned to the table with four tall glasses on a tray. She set it down and handed a glass to each of them. Crystal sipped, barely noticing the sweet coconut-pineapple combination.

Sarah leaned back in her chair and chatted to the men about the island and other things that Crystal didn't really hear because her heart thundered loudly as she wondered if she'd done the wrong thing in bringing Brent and Evan here. Maybe she'd become too comfortable . . . too certain that the men were hers no matter what.

Too arrogant.

Both Brent and Evan seemed captivated with Sarah, their attention fully on her as if Crystal didn't even exist.

A pang of irritation shot through her. Well, the hell with it. If they could be pulled from her so easily, that just proved they didn't have what it took to go the distance in a relationship with her. And at the same time, a little voice gnawed at her that she was overreacting. The men were simply paying attention to a pretty woman.

Crystal glanced at Sarah again. Okay, a fabulously stunning woman. It was only natural.

Still, it rankled.

She took a deep sip of her piña colada, feeling the burn of the rum in her throat, and she drew back her shoulders. She'd told Sarah she was willing to share Brent and Evan, if they agreed, and she wouldn't back down on that now.

Another sip of her drink and she realized it was empty.

"It looks like you could use a refill," Sarah said, and stood up.

"It's okay. I'll get it." Crystal stood and walked toward the bar, but Sarah followed her.

As Sarah filled her glass, she murmured, "You seem a bit nervous."

Crystal glanced at Sarah's jade green eyes. "I'm just . . . not sure how we'll get this started. No matter what we do, it seems it'll be really awkward."

Sarah's lips turned up in a devilish smile. "Not necessarily. Are you willing to follow my lead? No matter what I suggest?"

Thoughts of Kade appearing . . . of his huge erection that had haunted her fantasies . . .

"If it involves Kade, I . . ."

"Honey, I know you're not ready for that . . . yet. No, just the four of us."

Crystal stared into those jade eyes. She had no idea what Sarah would ask her to do, and that excited her. This was a chance to take a walk on the wild side. She nodded, then returned to the table and sat down.

Sarah returned to her chair but didn't sit down. She untied the sarong wrapped loosely around her hips, then drew it free. Brent's and Evan's gazes locked on her long, tanned legs. She turned around, revealing a perfectly rounded, heart-shaped derriere, left naked by her thong bikini. Her hips swayed seductively as she walked toward the pool.

Once there, she turned around. "You don't mind if I

go native, do you?" She reached behind her to the clasp on her bathing suit top and waited.

Of course, they'd already seen her topless, but something about being naked in a private yard made it seem much more intimate.

"Uh . . . I don't mind," Evan said.

Brent turned to Crystal with a questioning glance.

"Um . . . sure. Go for it," Crystal said.

They all watched in anticipation as Sarah's hands fiddled behind her back, then the top loosened slightly around her ribs. She smiled broadly, then turned around. With her back toward them, she slipped the thin bathing suit straps off her shoulders, then tossed the top onto the stone deck of the pool.

She stepped into the water and down a couple of steps until the glittering liquid swished around her calves, then she glanced back over her shoulder and smiled at them.

"Crystal, come and join me."

Crystal put down her drink and stood up, then untied the sash of her bathing suit cover-up and dropped it from her shoulders. She tossed it onto the chair and walked toward the swimming pool, feeling the men's hot gazes on her own thong-bared behind. Once she reached Sarah she stepped into the water, down two steps, and stood beside her.

Brent couldn't pull his gaze from Crystal's gorgeous ass, bare and round. Then Sarah turned around and he couldn't help staring at her full, round breasts, the nipples large and dusky rose. Man, the woman was gorgeous. No competition for Crystal, of course, who took his breath away every time he saw her, but Sarah was a phenomenally beautiful woman.

Sarah rested her hand on Crystal's shoulder, and Brent's breath caught. Would this . . . could this possibly go . . . where his swelling cock hoped it would go?

Beside him, Evan shifted in his chair, clearly entertaining the same fantasy.

"Crystal, honey, I meant join me in my freedom." Sarah's fingers glided to the back of Crystal's bikini top. Sarah turned, standing in profile, as she fiddled with the clasp. The curve of her firm breasts and her nipples pointing straight forward sent Brent's cock straining.

And Crystal didn't stop her.

Both men sucked in a breath as the clasp released and Crystal shrugged out of the top. Sarah tossed it on top of hers. Two colorful bits of cloth abandoned on the stone. Brent wished Crystal would turn around so he could see her lovely round breasts. His gaze fell to Sarah's and his heart rate increased. Slowly, Crystal turned around and her pert, round breasts, not as big as Sarah's but every bit as spectacular, came into view.

Crystal pulled her gaze from Sarah and raised it toward him, almost shyly. When their gazes caught, hers careened away immediately.

"Why don't you two come sit on the edge of the pool?" Sarah asked.

Brent shot to his feet at the same time as Evan, and they both moved to the side of the curved pool, positioning themselves so they could see the women straight on, and sat down. The water was cool on Brent's feet.

Sarah took Crystal's hand and led her into the water. As it swished against Crystal's abdomen, her nipples tightened, growing hard. Brent glanced at Sarah's full breasts. Her big, dusky nipples hardened, too.

Crystal followed Sarah deeper into the water. Her tight nipples ached, partly because of the cold, but mostly because of the attention of the two men watching them . . . and because of Sarah's avid interest. Sarah released Crystal's hand and swam into the deeper water. Crystal followed her to the far end of the pool and clung to the edge. Sarah urged her to the curved walkout steps in the deep end. Sarah's cool, delicate hand wrapped around Crystal's, and Sarah led her out of the water to the diving board.

"Sit," Sarah said.

Crystal sank onto the board, and Sarah's gaze drifted from Crystal's face to her shoulders, then downward. As the woman stared at Crystal's naked breasts, heat suffused her, warming her, belying the sharp point of her nipples. Crystal hazarded a glance toward the men. She caught Evan's intensely hot attention locked on her nipples. Crystal almost jumped as she felt Sarah's cool fingertips stroke across the swell of her breast, then over her hard nipple.

"You have beautiful breasts, Crystal."

Crystal's cheeks burned at the compliment. This was

so surreal. This woman touching her, looking at her as though she longed to fuck her silly, the two men looking on with rapt attention. She'd thought this was about Sarah being with the two men, but it had turned around on her.

She glanced at Brent, his hot gaze nearly searing her, then she got it. This was how Sarah wanted to get things rolling. What guy didn't fantasize about two women together? One woman touching another like this was guaranteed to get any man hot. Just as when Sarah had put suntan lotion on Crystal's naked breasts at the beach and vice versa.

But this was more intense. There was no pretense that it was innocent touching. Everything about this situation was sexually charged.

Sarah's fingers stroked over Crystal's other nipple, and heat pooled inside her. Sarah was getting Crystal very turned on. Sarah crouched down, and as her other hand stroked down Crystal's belly and along the thong strap encircling her waist, Crystal realized this wasn't just about Sarah getting fucked by the two men.

Crystal was about to go where she had never journeyed before.

Sarah leaned forward and her tongue teased Crystal's hard, aching nipple. One hand glided around to Crystal's back and drew her forward, while the other tucked around her breast. Suddenly, the cold nub was enveloped in the heat of Sarah's mouth, her tongue dabbing and teasing until Crystal's breathing grew erratic. Then that warm mouth moved to her other breast and sucked the nipple deep. Crystal gasped.

Sarah pressed her hand on Crystal's chest until she lay on her back.

"Move up," Sarah instructed.

Crystal glided farther onto the board, the rough finish abrading her back as she moved, adding to the intensely sensual feelings washing through her. As Sarah urged her farther still, Crystal drew her legs onto the board and pushed back until she lay fully stretched out.

Sarah rested a knee beside Crystal's waist and grabbed her wrists, pinning them above her head. Instinctively, Crystal pushed against the restraint, her chest arching upward.

Sarah leaned forward and captured Crystal's lips in a delicate kiss. Then she deepened it, her tongue gliding into Crystal's mouth. Taken aback, Crystal sucked in air, then the sweet sensation of a soft tongue nudging into her mouth, delicate lips playing on hers, seduced her into submission. She opened and allowed Sarah full access.

Sarah released Crystal's mouth, then kissed down her chest and covered her nipple. Then drew it deep. At the feel of the hot, moist mouth covering her and the deep pull on her aching nub, Crystal gasped again.

"I'm going to let go of your wrists," Sarah said with commanding authority. "When I do, hang on to the diving board and don't let go. Understand?"

Crystal nodded. When Sarah released her, she grasped the board on either side just above her head and hung on, which caused her chest to push upward a little. God, it felt incredibly sexy lying prone on the diving board with no idea what was coming next, especially with both men watching so intently, clearly turned on.

Sarah hooked her fingers under the elastic of Crystal's thong and drew it downward. Crystal glanced at the men as she lifted her hips so Sarah could guide the thong down her hips, thighs, and then off. Evan stroked the bulge in his bathing suit, while Brent steadfastly kept his hands curled in his lap.

Sarah guided one of Crystal's legs off one side of the diving board, then the other off the other side, so Crystal straddled the board. Opening her to Sarah. Sarah sat on the board and stroked Crystal's inner thighs. Crystal trembled at the delicate touch. Sarah laid both her hands flat on Crystal's legs and stroked upward, closing in on Crystal's melting center. Without thinking, Crystal let her fingers slip from the board.

Immediately, Sarah stood up and captured her wrists again.

"I think I might need help keeping this one in line." Sarah glanced toward the men. "Brent and Evan, would you give me a hand?"

# Sixteen

Crystal almost giggled as the men hurried toward her, but when their strong hands clamped around her wrists like iron bands and pinned her to the board again, her heart raced. She glanced up at Evan and he winked at her. When Sarah stroked Crystal's thighs again, her eyelids closed at the delicious sensations rushing through her.

Sarah's fingertips glided upward. Slowly. Getting closer to Crystal's aching vagina. Crystal arched upward. Delicate fingers. Skimming lightly along her sensitive flesh.

Then they touched her. There, where heat must surely be steaming from her. A soft sigh escaped her lips. Her entire focus centered on the fingers. Sliding along her slick flesh. Slipping inside her opening. Stroking. Deeper.

A warm mouth covered her clit and she gasped, then moaned as Sarah's tongue fluttered on her sensitive bud. Crystal pushed against the strong male hands imprisoning her wrists, then moaned in frustration and delight as the tongue fluttered again, then spiraled against her clit.

She bucked forward. Sarah laughed, a soft, melodious sound. Then she pressed down on Crystal's hips and pressed her mouth more firmly on Crystal's slit, then drove her fingers inside while sucking her clit. Wild sensations danced through Crystal as she arched and bucked again. Pleasure washed through her, increasing steadily until her moan turned into a cry of release as the waves of pleasure crested in shattering ecstasy.

Finally, she collapsed on the board, spent.

Sarah leaned forward and kissed her, then stood up. She peeled off her thong and tossed it aside, then settled her hands on her hips.

"Now, I want a couple of good men." She smiled and glanced toward Evan and Brent, who still held Crystal's wrists. "I think you two will do nicely."

Brent glanced at Crystal, his cock twitching inside his bathing suit as if trying to escape. Damn, that was the hottest thing he'd ever witnessed. Her face still glowed from her orgasm. He stroked her long, chestnut brown hair from her face. She smiled up at him and nodded. He glanced at Sarah, naked and sexy. This was why Crystal had brought them here.

He had to hand it to Crystal. She certainly showed a strong sense of self-esteem throwing Evan and him at this stunning woman. Brent found Crystal infinitely more attractive, but it was still true that Sarah was an incredibly beautiful woman. He was proud of Crystal for being so secure within herself.

Evan stripped off his T-shirt and bathing suit and tossed them aside in a heap. Brent followed suit, freeing his hard, straining cock. As Sarah watched them, she smiled and stroked her breasts, then tweaked her nipples to tight, hard buds.

"Brent, come over here and stroke my breasts."

He glanced down at Crystal and searched her expression again.

She smiled. "You're not going to ignore my Mistress, are you?"

Mistress? Oh, God, the sound of that made him hot. Sarah commanding Crystal. Making her perform sexual acts. His cock stiffened even more.

He stepped toward Sarah and rested his hand on her shoulder, his gaze glued to her hard nipples. He glided down her chest, then cupped her luscious breasts.

"Oh, that feels good," she said. "Evan, stand behind me and stroke me, too."

Evan stepped close behind her, his big cock jutting forward. Maybe it was because Brent's hormones were hyperactive from the erotic scene he'd just witnessed, but at the sight of Evan's huge erection, Brent had to fight an intense yearning to grab that cock and stroke it.

As Evan's hands glided around to Sarah's breasts, Brent shifted his hands upward to caress her soft face. Evan stroked her nipples, then covered her breasts with his hands.

Brent tipped her head up and kissed her, gliding his tongue over her delicate lips before pushing into her warm, moist mouth. He remembered how these lips had played over Crystal's breasts only moments before. Then over her delightful pussy. Giving Crystal pleasure. Bringing her to orgasm. His cock ached with need.

Evan's hands slid from Sarah's breasts, then he grasped her arms.

"We don't take orders from you," Evan said with mock disdain. "We can easily overpower you, so I suggest you do as *we* say."

Brent gazed into Sarah's eyes and saw a fire ignite.

"What if I refuse?" she tossed back at them.

Evan tightened his hold and drew her back against his solid, naked body. "You really have little choice."

As he pulled her arms back, Sarah's breasts arched forward. Brent stroked them, then leaned down and covered one with his mouth, then sucked. Hard. His cock twitched at her sharp gasp. He lifted his head and moved to her other nipple as Evan cupped the abandoned one and squeezed the nipple between his thumb and index finger. He caught a quick glimpse of Crystal, now sitting on the diving board, watching them. His cock swelled more as he noticed her fingers gliding between her legs and dipping inside her pussy. He sucked harder on Sarah's nipple and she moaned.

Oh, God, he was so fucking turned on.

Evan drew her backward, then pressed her head down, leaning her toward Brent. Brent grasped his hard cock and pressed it to her pink lips, then groaned as she wrapped them around his shaft. She licked the tip of him, then dove downward, taking him fully into her mouth and throat. She glided back and wrapped her delicate hands around him, then sucked his cockhead like a pacifier.

Brent's eyelids drifted closed, then jerked open when he realized he was picturing Evan sucking his cock. What the hell was wrong with him?

Evan strolled to the table and grabbed a condom, then ripped open the package and rolled it on. He grabbed an extra and returned, dropping it on the ground beside Brent. He stroked Sarah's round ass, then grasped his hard shaft and teased the opening with his tip, then moved lower and drove in deep. Sarah moaned around Brent's cockhead, then began to suck again. Evan thrust a few more times, then drew back. He repositioned himself, then very slowly eased forward.

Through a haze of lust, Brent watched Evan's cock slide into her back opening. God, he'd longed to do that to Crystal, but after she'd told him of her ex-husband's clumsy attempts, he had decided that the pleasure it would give him wasn't worth the anxiety it would cause Crystal.

But as he watched Evan's hard shaft glide between Sarah's beautiful round buttocks, all he could think of was Evan's cock. And his own pleasure as Sarah sucked and squeezed him.

Sarah's mouth slipped from Brent's cock. "Oh, God, yeah. I want your cock in my ass." She sucked in a breath as Evan slid deeper. "Ohhh . . . yeah. Push it in."

She threw her head back, her fingers tightening around Brent's erection, stroking him up and down, sending intense pleasure surging through him.

Evan pushed all the way in, impaling her. He grasped her hips and drew her to the end of the diving board, then sat down. Crystal scooted off the board to a nearby lounge chair, where she stretched out. Brent watched her glide her glistening fingers into her pussy again. He turned back to the woman sitting on Evan, her legs open wide. Evan's hands grasped her hips and he guided her up and down. The sight of his cock gliding in and out of her ass sent Brent's hormones spinning out of control.

He grabbed the condom from the ground and opened it, then rolled it on . . . Sarah's hungry gaze sending heat thrumming through him. He walked toward her, aching to feel her wet pussy around him. Grasping his cock, he knelt in front of her, then pressed his cockhead to her slick opening.

"Oh, yes," she murmured. "Drive your big cock into me."

All reasonable thought drifted from his brain as he drove forward into the slick heat of her body. She tightened around him. Her hands grasped his shoulders as his body pressed her tight against Evan. Evan's cock would be deep inside her ass, practically brushing against Brent's own cock.

Fuck, yeah, this was what he and Evan had fantasized about. Sharing a woman like this. It was erotic and wild and brought a whole new facet to their friendship.

An intimate, erotic facet. Almost as though he and Evan were fucking each other.

"Oh, please. Fuck me," Sarah whimpered.

Brent drew back, then thrust forward, embedding his cock into her again.

Crystal stroked her aching breast with one hand and glided her fingers deeper into her vagina as she watched Evan and Brent driving into Sarah. Watching the two cocks glide in and out of her, like flesh-and-blood pistons stoking her fire, sent Crystal into a spin. Sarah moaned, and Crystal's vagina clenched around her fingers. Their cocks drove into Sarah faster. Evan's face contorted in pleasure. Brent's perennially controlled expression faded a little.

Crystal found her clit and quivered her fingertip over it.

"Oh, God, yes. Fuck me harder." Sarah threw back her head and wailed as an orgasm washed over her. Within moments, both men groaned and shuddered against her.

The sight excited Crystal intensely, and her body tightened. Pleasure washed over her and she cried out, too, riding the wave.

Crystal collapsed into the chair, watching Sarah sag between Evan and Brent. They glanced over at Crystal, their gazes intense. Even though they were still inside Sarah, she could see their hunger. Brent turned back to Sarah and kissed her, then drew away from her and stripped off the condom. Within moments, he stood in front of Crystal. He lifted her from the chair and carried her to the grass, then settled over her. His cock was semi-erect as he lowered himself onto her and captured her lips in a passionate kiss. His tongue swept inside her mouth, taking her breath away. His cock, resting against her belly, hardened. She wrapped her hand around his shaft and

stroked until it was rock hard, then guided it to her opening. He drove into her again and again, until waves of
pleasure pummeled her to pure ecstasy, followed by his
groan of completion. She clung to his shoulders and
moaned long and hard.

After a few minutes, he slowed and then smiled down
at her. His kiss was sweet and loving this time, then he
drew away. Evan stepped toward her, hunger in his eyes.
He prowled over her, then pressed his rock-hard cock to
her opening and drove inside. His cock filled her again
and again, and she immediately moaned in yet another
orgasm. Evan followed right behind her.

God, these men knew how to fuck her.

Evan kissed her, then rolled to one side and held her
close.

Crystal had been worried she'd be jealous, but the
sight of her two men fucking Sarah actually gave her more
confidence. Because it was clear that as much as they
seemed to enjoy Sarah, they wanted Crystal more.


Crystal sipped her drink as she sat stretched out on the
lounge chair, watching the sensational sunset over the
ocean. The sky was awash in orange and golden streaks,
deep orange reflected in the rippling water. Brent sat in
the chair next to her, and Evan stood beside a tall potted
plant, gazing over the water.

None of them had spoken much since this afternoon's
encounter with Sarah. Brent and Evan had certainly enjoyed the sexual escapade, but once they'd returned to

the villa, it was as if reality had set in and they weren't sure how to react to what had happened. She'd gone for a swim in the pool, then done some reading, leaving them to their thoughts. Brent had pulled together a delicious salad with tangy marinated chicken for dinner, and now they quietly enjoyed the spectacular end to the day.

But it was just after seven, with several hours to go before bedtime. She couldn't let this silence linger.

"So neither of you has said much this evening," she said.

Evan turned his head toward her but said nothing, then took a sip of beer from the tall glass he held.

She turned to Brent. "You did enjoy being with Sarah, didn't you?"

Brent glanced at her, then back to the sunset. "Yeah. Sure."

Her eyebrow arched. "Neither of you seems very enthusiastic."

Evan glanced at Brent uncertainly, then back to Crystal. "Well, it was a little strange. Being with another woman. In front of you."

She rested her hand on her chest, her fingers stroking the skin between her bikini-clad breasts. "I found it *very* exciting. Especially with you two sharing her." She smiled.

Brent stood up. "I'm going to go clean up those dishes."

"Really?" She watched as he picked up his empty glass and headed for the patio door. Brent volunteering to do dishes?

"I'll help." Evan glanced at Crystal's glass, which was almost empty. "You want another cooler?"

She finished the last sip and handed him the glass. "Sure."

He disappeared into the house. Five minutes later, he appeared with a new drink for her, then sat down.

"I thought you were going to help."

"I was, but I think Brent needs a little space right now."

She pursed her lips. "Was it a mistake suggesting the two of you share Sarah?"

Evan sipped his beer, then sat back in the chair. "Not as far as I'm concerned. I'm going to fantasize about this afternoon for a long time to come." He turned his heated gaze her way. "Especially the part where Sarah was licking your pussy."

She laughed. Men were all the same that way. At least, she'd thought so. She glanced toward the house.

"So why is Brent unhappy? Do you think he feels guilty, even though I said it was okay?"

"Maybe. I'm not really sure. I tried to talk to him about it in the kitchen, but he just closed up. I have no doubt he was into it—I mean, his cock was rock hard—but . . ." Evan shrugged.

Crystal leaned back in the chair and gazed at the sunset. She'd just have to wait and see if Brent would open up about it later.

She and Evan relaxed on the patio, watching the blazing sky as the sun sank below the horizon. Soon it turned dark, and they decided to go into the house. The kitchen counters were sparkling clean, and Brent sat in front of the TV.

"Want to join me?" he asked, patting the couch cushion beside him.

She glanced at the screen and the flashing explosions. An adventure movie of some sort.

"I will." Evan sat in the armchair and put his feet up on the ottoman.

"No, I guess I'll go read my book." She headed for the bedroom. She'd give them a while alone. Maybe Evan could talk to him and find out what was up.

Two hours later, she stuck her head back into the living room to see them both still engrossed in the TV. Some car chase this time. She should have known better than to think two guys would talk about *feelings,* especially with an exciting movie on TV.

She went back to the bedroom and pulled on her slinkiest black nightgown, the one that hugged her body, plunged deep at the neckline, with a slit up one leg to the hip. She sashayed into the living room and posed in the doorway, a hand on one hip, the other resting against the door frame.

Neither of them looked her way, so she stepped into the room with a sway to her hips, then sat on the couch beside Brent. As she crossed her legs, the nightgown fell open, revealing her long, tanned thigh.

Brent glanced in her direction, then his gaze locked on her naked leg. She stroked her thigh, aware that Evan had glanced her way, too. Both men watched the motion avidly.

"I was thinking that maybe tonight we could all go to bed together."

She glanced up at Brent, and her heart sank as she saw hesitation in his eyes. Then his gaze shifted to the swell of her breasts, and he grabbed her hand and stood up.

He practically dragged her across the room and down the hall.

"Coming, Evan?" Brent called as he strode into the bedroom.

"Right behind you, buddy."

# Seventeen

Damn. Ever since Crystal stepped into the living room in that sexy, curve-hugging nightgown, Brent's cock had been aching. Now, at the sight of her smiling at him while she turned and stroked her hands down her sides, gliding over the shiny black fabric, his swollen cock throbbed with need. He wanted to fling his arms around her and press her onto the bed, then sink his hard shaft into her.

But that's not what she wanted. Not exactly. She wanted both him and Evan to fuck her at the same time. To push both their cocks into her at the same time.

But they'd done exactly that with Sarah this afternoon, and the whole thing had left Brent . . . unnerved. He'd had feelings . . . disturbing feelings . . . about Evan. Crap, a beautiful, exceptionally sexy woman had been between them, moaning in the throes of passion . . . and Brent had felt a deep desire to touch Evan, for God's sake. To grab his cock and stroke it.

He'd wanted that big erection in his hand. And he'd

wanted Evan to touch him, too. To feel Evan's strong hands around his cock. Squeezing. Pulsing it in his hand.

God, and more, but he wouldn't even let his thoughts go there.

Crystal slid one strap off her shoulder. In a minute, she'd be standing in front of them naked.

Damn it. If the three of them got busy right now, he'd have to face those feelings again, and he just couldn't handle that right now.

He stepped toward Crystal and stilled her hand as she reached for the other strap.

"Wait."

She gazed up at him, her eyes wide in surprise.

He needed a little time. These confusing feelings were probably just a result of the excitement and strangeness of the situation. Somehow his hormones had crossed wires. That's all. Tomorrow, he'd have everything more in perspective. But tonight . . .

"It's been an eventful day," Brent continued. "Why don't we just . . . sleep?"

She gazed at him for a moment, then sighed and nodded. "Okay, sure." She turned to the bed and bit her lower lip. "I was really hoping . . ." She glanced back to him. "I really wanted to be close to both of you. I was hoping we could all . . . sleep together. But I don't want you to be uncomfortable."

Evan glanced at Brent, then shrugged and moved toward the bed.

"Come on. It's a big bed," Evan said. "There's room for all of us."

Brent stared at the bed as Evan pulled back the covers, then shed his clothing, revealing a thick, purple-veined boner. Brent tried to pry his gaze from his friend's erection but couldn't do it. His own cock swelled even more.

Damn it, he wasn't attracted to men. He was in love with Crystal, for God's sake.

Crystal gazed at Brent uncertainly. If he backed away now, she would climb into bed with Evan and there was no way in hell they wouldn't wind up fucking. Not if Brent left them alone. And it wasn't even about that. Evan seemed to be able to handle Crystal's taste for exploring the wild side, and Brent knew he ran the risk that Crystal might wind up choosing Evan over him because of that. But he loved her, and he didn't want to lose her.

The crazy thing was, he found Crystal's wild side intensely appealing. He loved that she wanted to try these unconventional and erotic adventures. But he had to get his head on straight and figure out what the hell was going on with these weird urges.

And the best way to do that was just to forge ahead. All they were talking about right now was sleeping in the same bed. Him and Crystal and Evan. With Crystal between them.

He could do that.

Sucking in a deep breath, Brent stripped off his clothes and followed Crystal to the bed, then climbed in beside her.

———

Crystal smiled as both men lay down beside her, one on either side. They both shifted close, but they remained on their backs, with only the sides of their bodies touching hers. She closed her eyes and wondered how long it would take to fall asleep, knowing there were two handsome hunks, both men she loved, lying naked beside her, both hot and hungry for her, even though they refused to act on it.

She sighed and closed her eyes.

An hour later she could tell they were still awake, but she finally felt herself drifting off.

Evan stared at the ceiling. Damn it. Would this night ever end?

Crystal lay beside him, her even breathing an indication that she had finally fallen asleep. And beside her was Brent. What was going on with Brent? They'd often talked about what a great adventure it would be to share a woman, yet ever since they'd done just that this afternoon, Brent had closed up. Evan understood that it must be odd for Brent having done it with Crystal watching, but that didn't feel like the issue. It felt more like Brent was angry at Evan for some reason.

He drew in a deep, even breath. What the hell did he expect? He had ruined his friend's wedding and, potentially, his happiness. Guilt dug through him, but deep down he knew—they all knew—that if they had hidden the fact that he and Crystal had feelings for each other, it would eventually have blown up in their faces. As painful as it was, it was better to bring it into the open and face it head-on.

Crystal murmured in her sleep, and her arm brushed his hip as she shifted position. His cock stood at full attention. How could it not with the feel of Crystal's warm body against his side, only a thin film of silk between them, and the knowledge that her soft breasts were within easy reach? He wanted to roll on his side and hug her close. To kiss her and explore her sexy curves.

But not with Brent there beside her.

Time continued to crawl by, but finally exhaustion kicked in and he dozed off.

*Crystal's body felt heavy with need. Evan's hands curled around her and stroked her breasts, making the nipples stand up hard and ache. He rolled her onto her side, away from him, and pressed his long, hard cock to her back opening. She sucked in a breath as he pushed forward, gliding deep inside her. She gasped at the intense pleasure of being filled by him.*

*She opened her eyelids, and Brent gazed at her with loving eyes.*

*"Can you feel Evan's big cock inside you?"*

*She nodded, squeezing her muscles around it.*

*"Do you like it?" Brent asked.*

*"Oh, yes," she replied, her voice hoarse.*

*"Good." Brent kissed her, and her insides melted with slick desire.*

*She loved Evan inside her, but she wanted more. She wanted Brent, too.*

He wrapped his hand around his big, hard cock and eased closer. She felt his solid erection press against her vagina and she opened for him, desperate to feel his big cock inside her, too.

He thrust forward and she moaned. His hot, marble-hard cock filled her. Both men's bodies pressed snugly against her, their long erections spiking into her. She sucked in air, trying to catch her breath, but the excitement flooding through her made that impossible.

"Oh, God, I can't believe you're both inside me. That you're both going to make love to me at the same time."

Brent kissed her while Evan's lips nuzzled the back of her neck.

"That's right, baby." Brent's mouth brushed hers again. "We're going to fuck you until you can't breathe. We're going to drill you until you scream in ecstasy."

"Oh, yes, do it! Please do it." She gasped as both cocks drove in deep. "Fuck me. Fuck me! FUCK ME!"

Her pleasure soared as they thrust into her—again and again. Rising like the incoming tide. Pounding through her.

But then it hit a plateau. They continued to fill her with their glorious cocks, but the crest of ecstasy never came.

She squirmed and threw her head back.


Light blasted through her eyelids and they flickered open. The feel of the big, hard cocks inside her faded. She squeezed internal muscles, hoping to ride the wave to completion, but to no avail.

She became aware of Evan's face on the pillow next to hers, his eyes closed. He was asleep.

Damn it. It had all been a dream.

Well, not all. She did have two sexy naked men in bed with her, but the part where they were fucking her was a dream.

She glanced at the clock: 6:10.

She grinned. Maybe it was a dream, but it was one she intended to make come true.

Brent woke up to the erotic feel of something warm and moist wrapped around his cock, which was swelling rapidly. Without opening his eyes, he reached down and stroked Crystal's hair as she sucked on his now hard cock. She kissed up his belly, then lapped at one of his nipples, which became bead hard under her flicking tongue. She sucked, sending burning heat through him, and he groaned. She shifted, and he opened his eyes and smiled.

Then his smile turned to a frown at the sight of Evan lying behind Crystal as she rolled onto her back and stretched out between them.

But his cock throbbed in need.

He shifted onto his side to face her, and she turned toward him with a smile. She cupped his cheek and leaned forward to nibble his whisker-roughened chin. Then she kissed him. He wrapped his arm around her and pulled her close to his body, trying to ignore the sight of Evan, who had moved close behind her and was kissing her shoulder. Her soft breasts compressed against Brent's chest, driving him wild. He tucked his hand around her head and kissed her, driving his tongue inside her mouth. Her tongue undulated against his, then he felt Evan's hand slide between their bodies and capture her nipple. A shiver rippled through Brent at Evan's touch. Her mouth slid away from his as she sucked in a breath. Then she groaned.

Brent stroked down her side, then his hand glided over her stomach to her thigh. But as he found her sweet pussy, his fingers brushed against something hard.

Evan's bulbous cockhead pushed between her thighs, and right now it rested in Brent's palm. Solid and thick.

An overwhelming desire to squeeze it . . . to wrap his hand around Evan's cock and stroke its length . . . raged through Brent. Oh, God, he wanted it so bad.

Brent jerked back. "God damn it!" His stomach clenched as he flung away the covers and bolted to his feet, then strode from the room.

# Eighteen

Crystal watched him go with wide eyes. Oh, God, had she ruined everything?

"Should we go after him?" she asked Evan, whose cock still sat snuggly between her legs, resting against her very slick, and aching, slit.

Evan squeezed her breast gently, drawing her back against him.

"No, he needs some space right now."

"What about you?" Her intense desire, stoked by being sandwiched between two hot, naked hunks all night, and an extremely erotic dream, made it difficult to concentrate. She flattened Evan's hand on her breast and leaned into it. Her nipple thrust into his palm. "You don't need any space?"

"I need as little space as possible between us right now." He guided her around to face him.

She immediately missed his big, hard cock so close to her wet, needy flesh. She stroked away the errant strands of hair that hung in his eyes and meshed her lips with his, then dipped her tongue into his mouth and tasted him.

"Oh, God, me, too." She wrapped her hand around his thick cock and stroked, imagining it gliding inside her, then slid her tongue into his mouth again.

He pressed her onto her back and prowled over her.

"Woman, you're driving me insane." He slipped his hand around hers and guided his cock to her opening. Then he teased her, gliding the tip over her slick opening but not pushing inside.

"Damn it, Evan. Push that thing inside me before I scream in frustration."

She drew her hand from his and dragged her fingertips over his balls to entice him.

He grinned. "I do intend to hear you scream, but frustration's not what I have in mind."

He nuzzled her neck, seemingly ignoring her demand while he continued to stroke her with the tip of his erection—then he shifted and drove into her. His hard shaft filled her like a thick, erotic stake, his body pinning her to the bed. She whimpered at the intense pleasure.

He grasped her wrists, pinned them above her head, and grinned down at her. "So? Is that what you wanted?"

She shimmied under him. "Almost." Then she squeezed her internal muscles around him, dragging a delightful groan from him. She nuzzled his temple, then blew in his ear. "Now fuck me."

"Yes, ma'am!" He drew back, then drove in deep again.

This time she groaned.

"Oh, God, give me more," she cried.

He drew back and thrust again. Then again. A few more thrusts of his hot, hard cock and joy catapulted through her. She moaned as she pushed against his hold on her wrists, the feeling of being restrained heightening her pleasure.

He kept thrusting, then arched his pelvis against her. Heat filled her as he groaned.

She relaxed and opened her eyes to see Evan staring at her intently. He captured her lips in a passionate kiss.

"God, I love you so much." He kissed her again. "I want you to be mine, to spend your life with me."

Her heart clenched. "Oh, Evan, I love you, too, but . . ." She couldn't keep staring into those deep green eyes of his. She rolled out from under him and buried her face in the pillow and groaned, tears prickling at her eyes. "I don't want to choose between you and Brent."

Evan settled beside her. She felt his hand stroke her shoulder, the contact gentle and reassuring.

"I know you love Brent, too. I get that. I don't know if it helps, but if you choose me, I would be happy—no, make that thrilled—to have Brent join us anytime you want."

She turned and gazed at him over her shoulder. "Really? You mean in bed?"

"Of course. I find it hot watching him make love to you. Bringing you pleasure. We'd have to work on the threesome thing—clearly we still have issues there—but I'm game."

Evan would let the three of them continue together. If she chose him. If she *married* him. If she chose Brent, however, would he agree to allow Evan into their relationship? And would Evan agree to that?

"You're thinking pretty hard. I hope that's a good sign." He smiled and captured her lips. "Now let's go have some breakfast."

Brent leaned against a palm tree as he gazed out over the glistening turquoise water edged by a white sandy beach. When he'd raced out of the bedroom this morning, he'd grabbed some shorts and a shirt from his luggage in the guest room and jumped in the rental car. Then he'd driven, mindlessly following the road until he'd wound up here, on yet another of the gorgeous beaches the island offered.

The sun beat down on him, and the breeze caressed his face. He sucked in a deep breath, then started to walk.

Damn, here he was in this tropical paradise on what was supposed to be his honeymoon with Crystal but had turned out to be a honeymoon for three. He'd shared a lot of things with his best friend, and the thought of sharing a woman with him had always been a turn-on, but with the reality had come the disturbing truth that . . . damn it, could he really be attracted . . . sexually . . . to his best friend?

Damn it, he should go back and demand that Crystal choose between the two of them right now. She couldn't have both of them. Not when sharing her meant being close to Evan, too. Possibly touching Evan, as he had this morning.

It's funny that when he'd fantasized about sharing a woman with Evan in the past, he'd never thought that part through.

Brent sucked in a breath. He and Evan had always been close friends. And he hoped that despite the fact they were competing for the same woman, they could continue to be close.

But not that close.

God damn it, if he kept up this behavior, he was going to ruin his chances with Crystal for good. Clearly, she wanted a partner who was open to new experiences, and Evan had been demonstrating that trait. And Brent had to admit, it was a huge turn-on watching her with Evan. At first, he'd thought that was because anything that gave Crystal sexual pleasure was a turn-on to him. Like watching her with Sarah. That had been hot beyond belief.

He stopped walking and turned to face the ocean, pushing his hands in his pockets.

But now he realized it was more than that. As disturbing as it was, he seemed to be turned on by Evan. Maybe his desire to share a woman with Evan had really been a desire to be with Evan all along. Sharing a woman had just been an excuse. And the reason they had never done it was that even though some part of him might want to be with Evan, he just wasn't ready for something like that.

Damn it, he really didn't understand this. He loved Crystal. He had no doubt about that. Why, then, did he have this growing desire to share sexual intimacy with Evan?

His fists clenched at his sides. No matter what happened on this vacation, or with his attitudes about sex *and his best friend,* Brent knew that the only important thing was that he won Crystal back. He needed her to choose him.

Because he loved her with all his heart.

Which was why it had been such a stupid move to fly out of there this morning, leaving her in bed, *naked,* with Evan. He knew she'd been extremely turned on, so there was no doubt in his mind that Evan had made love to her after he'd left.

He shook his head and stared over the vast ocean in front of him. The thought should make him angry, but things were so screwed up . . . emotions all around in such turmoil . . . it just made him realize what a mess this was.

He and Evan had been friends for a long time, and they'd shared a lot of confidences, supported each other through breakups, job problems, family issues, and more. If he needed someone, he always knew he could depend on Evan. That made this whole thing with Evan falling in love with Crystal even more difficult.

He dug his sandaled toe into the sand. The thing was, he understood Evan's point of view. Brent had had the same dilemma when he'd met Crystal years before. She was already engaged at the time, and he had longed to be with her. Sure, he hadn't done anything about it, but he hadn't gotten to know her back then as Evan had in these past two years. Ever since Brent started dating Crystal, the three of them had spent a lot of time together. They'd become very close. If Brent had been paying more attention, he would have realized that the growing friendship between Crystal and Evan had been turning into something more. Brent had to admire the fact that Evan had held off so long.

He'd believed Evan when he'd said he hadn't intended to act on his attraction at all. As the wedding day had grown close, however, Brent couldn't really blame Evan for finally falling prey to his own desire for happiness and at least telling her how he felt. Crystal deserved the right to make up her own mind, and she had. If Brent hadn't been a fool and walked away, then Crystal would have married him that day. He couldn't blame Evan for what had happened.

Now Crystal had to sort out her feelings. He had to admit, he didn't want to win her just because she felt obligated to follow up on her promise to marry him. He wanted her to want him the most.

But she seemed to be in love with both of them.

And Brent really didn't want to give up his friendship with Evan, which seemed sure to happen no matter how this went.

Unless there was some way to figure out how to let the loser not actually be a loser. If Crystal chose Brent, could he get past his issues about being in an intimate situation with Evan and invite Evan to continue their erotic adventures? If Crystal was his wife, Brent could get over the feeling that Evan was a threat to his happiness. Would Evan consider such an arrangement?

———

Crystal and Evan ate a breakfast of fruit and croissants on the patio as they enjoyed the incredible view of the ocean glittering in the sunlight, the dazzling white sand of the beach, and a vivid blue sky devoid of clouds. Brent still hadn't returned after another hour, so they decided to continue their plans to go swimming with the stingrays, something Crystal had been anticipating since she'd won this trip. Renee had told her about a place where they could stand in waist-deep water and the tame, almost pet-like stingrays would swarm around them, then they could feed the rays by hand. Renee had suggested a great tour company and had booked their excursion ahead of time.

The breeze flowed through Crystal's hair, blowing it back off her face as she and Evan rode the boat with several other tourists to the sandbar. She couldn't stop worrying about Brent and how he'd stormed out this morning. This whole situation was very difficult for him. For all of them. She really needed to choose, but how could she do that? She loved them both.

God, she didn't want to hurt either one of them. She just prayed that somehow, no matter what the outcome, they'd be able to find a way to make their long-term friendship work.

Finally, the boat arrived at the shallow sandbar and Crystal climbed down the boat ladder into the warm ocean water, followed by Evan. The bottom was soft and sandy and the shallow water crystal clear. As soon as she caught sight of the large, graceful creatures swimming toward them, Crystal laughed with joy and set aside her worries and simply enjoyed this wonderful experience.

The rays swam right up to her, then one bumped against her. Soon she was surrounded by them, as were the others in the group of fifteen or so people on the tour.

"That's how they tell you they would like some food," said Henri, one of the tour guides. He had hopped into the water right along with them and circulated around to talk to each of his clients. He handed her a hunk of white meat. She held it in the water, and one of the large creatures raced toward her hand and sucked the meat from her fingers. Its belly was velvety soft as it brushed against her.

After a delightful time interacting with the friendly stingrays, she and Evan boarded the boat again with the others and sailed to a nearby reef. In the clear water, the two of them enjoyed swimming among the brightly colored fish and even spotted a large moray eel.

When they finally returned to shore, Crystal was tired but happy. When they reached their rental car, Evan opened the passenger door for her and she stretched out in the seat, glad he had volunteered to drive back to the villa.

"You're awfully quiet. Did you have a good time today?" he asked.

She glanced at Evan's handsome profile as he drove. "Sure. It was fantastic. I loved it."

But even to her ears the enthusiasm sounded strained. She had enjoyed the day, it was true, but now her thoughts had returned to Brent. For months, Crystal had been looking forward to swimming with the stingrays, and Brent had been just as excited about it as she had. She'd imagined sharing the experience with him. Now she wouldn't get the chance. As much as she'd loved spending the time with Evan, she'd missed having Brent by her side.

As soon as Crystal stepped in the door, she glanced around for Brent, but he wasn't in the living room. The other car was in the driveway, so he should be here. She walked toward the back of the house and peered out the patio door, but he wasn't in the back, either.

"He might be taking a nap." Evan leaned against the kitchen doorway, watching her.

She nodded, feeling a little sheepish, as though she were cheating on Evan by missing Brent.

As if reading her thoughts, he strolled forward and rested his hand on her arm. "It's okay. I get it. He stormed out of here this morning, now you're worried about him."

She nodded, then walked down the hallway toward the master bedroom, immediately noticing that both bedroom doors were open. She stole a quick glance in the guest bedroom as she walked by, but Brent was not there. She went into the master bedroom and through to the en suite bathroom, where she pulled her wet bathing suit and towel from her bag and hung them over the shower door to dry.

As she walked down the hall again, she heard Evan's voice.

"Crystal, Brent just came in the backyard. He must have been at the beach."

# Nineteen

Crystal hurried to the patio door and peeked out to see Brent, a towel tossed carelessly around his neck and his hair wet and tousled, walking past the pool toward the house. Her heart pounded.

"Evan . . ." She glanced toward him. "I really need to talk to Brent. Do you think . . . ?" Damn, how did she ask him to make himself scarce?

"Yeah, sure. I can find something to do with myself."

He walked through the house to the living room. She stepped to the doorway between the kitchen and the living room and watched him grab a set of keys from the bowl by the door.

"I'll probably be back about eleven. I assume I'll be sleeping alone." He opened the door.

He was cooperating, but clearly not happy.

"Evan."

He paused and glanced back.

"Thanks for understanding."

He nodded, then closed the door behind him.

Brent walked across the patio, the stone slabs hot under his bare feet. When he'd returned to the villa this afternoon, Crystal and Evan hadn't been there. Then he'd remembered that this had been the day they had scheduled the trip to see the stingrays.

His stomach twisted as he remembered how excited Crystal had been about that, and how often they'd talked about it. Anticipated it. Then he'd taken off this morning, leaving Evan to share that unique experience with her. To share memories that would last a lifetime.

Damn, but he really needed to get his act together, or he'd lose her.

Rather than sitting in the lonely house, he'd gone for a walk on the beach, then enjoyed a swim in the warm ocean water. He slid open the patio door and stepped inside the cool house.

"Brent."

He glanced at the doorway to the kitchen to see Crystal watching him.

"Crystal, honey, I'm sorry about missing the stingrays today."

She shook her head. "No, it's okay. I understand. You needed your space, you needed—"

"I needed to be with you. I needed to show you I want to do the things we've dreamed of doing together."

She stepped toward him and glided her hand lightly along his upper arm, almost as if she were afraid he'd disappear again. She shook her head. "A silly trip is not important, not in the scheme of things. What's important is that I love you. And I was afraid that with what happened this morning . . . well, over this whole trip"—she gazed at him, her eyes glimmering—"that I'd driven you away."

He grabbed her shoulders and pulled her into a kiss, reveling in the feel of her soft lips under his. "You'll never drive me away."

She gazed up at him uncertainly.

"Ever." He captured her mouth again, and this time her arms came around him and she melted into his embrace.

He opened as her tongue slipped inside and glided over his. His groin tightened at the sweet intimacy. She pushed her tongue deeper, then slid her hand down his chest, heading for his steadily swelling cock. Longing to feel her fingers wrap around him . . . to feel her soft body open to him as he glided inside her . . . grew to an excruciating need.

He drew his mouth from hers.

"Where's Evan?"

"He's gone out."

Relief washed through him. After walking and thinking all afternoon, Brent had finally realized that he had to come to terms with whatever was going on inside him in relation to Evan. Maybe the urges he'd experienced were just a normal part of being in a heightened sexual situation, or maybe there was something more going on, but no matter which was the case, Brent needed to face it head-on.

Brent smiled and scooped Crystal into his arms.

But not right now.

Evan returned around eleven. He'd driven along an ocean-view road for a while, then stopped at a nice little restaurant with a bar overlooking the ocean. He'd had a couple of drinks, then ordered dinner. After that, he'd killed some time walking along the beach, watching the moonlight glitter on the water, and allowing the ocean waves to wash away his worries.

Now that he was back at the villa, however, they came crashing back. He kicked off his shoes and walked down the hall. The master bedroom door was closed. Of course, it would be. Because Crystal was in there with Brent.

And he was outside. Isolated and alone.

He closed the other bedroom door behind him and flopped on the bed. Damn it, it was torture knowing Crystal was in there with Brent, while he was in here. He kept expecting Crystal to suddenly realize that Brent was the one she wanted and cut Evan out of the relationship. After all, she had already agreed to marry Brent. She'd been confused for a while, but it was clear when she looked at Brent that she was in love with him.

Just when Evan had started to believe that he had an edge, because he shared Crystal's desire to explore the wild situations they discovered, he realized that those were just fleeting whims. Something she wanted to do

while here on the island, but once they returned home—
when she finally had to choose between them . . . Damn.
He flung his arm over his eyes.

Deep down, he knew she'd choose Brent.


Crystal heard Evan's steps in the hallway, then the other
bedroom door close. She glanced at Brent, his face inches
from hers on the pillow. He stroked her hair back from
her face, the delicate touch sending tingles through her.

"I know you don't want to hurt either one of us," he
said.

"I don't." She ran her finger along his cheek. "And I
know how close the two of you are. I don't want to see
your friendship end, either."

He grinned. "And you're hot for him."

She smiled at his teasing tone, but then his eyes grew
serious.

"You know how much I love you."

She nodded.

"I can't imagine you not in my life. I hope and pray
that you choose me to be your husband."

He leaned in close and kissed her. When he released
her lips, she gazed into his warm brown eyes.

"I know that in order to choose between us, you
need to explore your feelings for Evan, and as part of that
you want to be with both of us." He smiled and stroked
her cheek. "And I have to admit, that's really hot. So, I
might have been a bit reluctant at first, but now I'm willing to push past my comfort zone and go for it."

"Are you sure? Because I don't want you to—"

His mouth covered hers and his tongue slid inside and swirled around, stealing her breath. He drew back and grinned at her wickedly. "You're not rescinding the offer of me making love to you in a hot, sexy threesome, are you?" He nibbled the curve of her neck with his lips. "You're not going to deny me watching Evan's big cock slide into you while I suck on your pert, hard nipples?"

Her nipples hardened at his words and her insides tightened.

"Well, when you put it like that . . ." She smiled and he captured her lips again, then he prowled over her, pinning her between his knees as he stared down at her like a predator about to consume her.

"Should we start now?" He grinned wickedly. "I can go get him."

Her gaze drifted down to his big, hard cock as it twitched in excitement. "No, I think right now"—she glided her hand down his muscular chest, then wrapped her hand around his impressive erection—"you're all I can handle."

Brent's smile widened and he leaned forward and nuzzled the base of her neck, sending ripples of pleasure careening through her. Then he grabbed her wrists and pinned them above her head. "I was hoping you'd say that."

As he kissed down her chest, heading for her aching breast, she sighed. He was such a good man, and she couldn't imagine not having him in her life. But was there room in their relationship for Evan? Or after their honeymoon for three, would they go back to the way things were and pretend none of this ever happened?

Brent's mouth glided over her nipple, shaking loose her thoughts and dragging her focus squarely on the pleasure rippling through her.


Crystal opened the door to the back patio and stepped into the bright sunshine and the warm tropical breeze. Brent sat on a chair by the pool, reading a magazine. With a wide grin, she stepped in front of him, blocking the sun. Brent had said he wanted to try to make things work with the three of them, so she intended to help.

He put down his magazine and glanced at her. "Hi. What's up?"

She flung open her robe, revealing her totally naked body beneath.

"Well, I'm hoping *you* are," she said.

His jaw dropped and his gaze fell to her breasts, then a slow smile spread across his face. She could see his swim trunks tenting.

"With you like that, I'm *up* for anything."

"I'm glad you put it that way," she said as she stepped toward him, a purposeful sway to her hips. She reached for his hand, then closed her fingers around his and coaxed him to his feet. "Follow me."

She led him to the elegant concrete bench that sat among lovely tropical flowers on the other side of the pool. She tossed the beach towel she'd brought with her onto the hard concrete. "Drop your trunks and sit there."

He grinned. "Whatever you say."

She licked her lips as he revealed his big, hard cock. The trunks slipped away and fell to the stone surface under his feet. God, it was long and thick, and she felt a little intimidated by the thought of it pushing inside her back opening. But she shook away those feelings, knowing she wanted him inside her there. Where he'd never been before.

She pulled the bottle of lube from her robe pocket and handed it to him. He glanced at the bottle, then his gaze caught hers, concern in his warm brown eyes.

He took the bottle. "Are you sure?"

She understood his reluctance. When he'd broached the subject of having anal sex about a year ago, she'd told him she wasn't comfortable with the idea. She'd told him that it hadn't worked well for her in the past.

But Sarah's pep talk on the beach had alleviated a lot of her anxieties about trying anal sex again. She knew Brent would be gentle and patient, and Sarah had told her it was very pleasurable. And just the thought of Brent's big cock inside her at the same time as Evan's made her insides melt.

"I want to feel you inside me in a way I never have before."

She allowed the robe to drop from her shoulders, then fall to the ground. She stroked her breasts. His gaze lay firmly on her fingers as she squeezed her nipples.

She leaned forward and kissed him, then glided her tongue along his lips. She dipped inside his warm mouth, tasting coffee, then drew back and kissed down his chest toward his nipple. When she licked it and sucked it in her mouth, he inhaled sharply. She teased it, then sucked deeply a couple of times, to his accompanying groans. Continuing downward, she lapped at his sculpted abs, then wrapped her hand around his warm, marble-hard cock and stared at it.

"Your cock is so gorgeous." She licked the end. "It's big and beautiful."

She licked it again, then took the cockhead in her mouth. His hand stroked through her hair as she sucked, then squeezed, loving the feel of the hard flesh filling her mouth. She glided back and released it, still holding his shaft in her hand, then she gazed at him.

"I want to feel it inside me from behind. And I'd like Evan to join us. I want both of you to make love to me at the same time." She kissed him. "Are you okay with that?"

At his hesitation, her heart clenched. Had she made a mistake? Had he changed his mind? Or maybe she'd mis-understood what he'd said last night.

Brent quelled his sudden flash of anxiety. Crystal was act-ing as a result of his declaration last night that he wanted to do this. Maybe he should have told her why he was struggling with this. Why the thought of taking this step was so difficult for him. But he didn't know how she'd react to his feelings for Evan. Would she feel confused or uncertain by them? Would she feel a little left out? Or would she just take it all in stride?

He could drive himself crazy with all this thinking. The only way to get through this was to be true to himself and go with the flow.

He smiled, then tucked his finger under her chin and tipped it up.

"Let's do this."

# Twenty

Crystal turned toward the house and waved. She could vaguely see Evan, who had been waiting for her signal, peering out at her. He nodded, then disappeared from the window. As she smiled at Brent and took the bottle of lube from his hand, she heard the patio door slide open.

She opened the plastic bottle and squeezed a generous amount on Brent's cock, then lovingly spread it on him. Over his mushroom-shaped head, down and around his long, hard shaft, around the base. Then she applied a little more on his tip. She leaned back, admiring his sculpted cock glistening in the sunlight.

"Now what?" he asked.

"Well, now you stand up and I'll do this." She leaned over and rested her hands on the bench, spreading her legs wide. A movement caught her eye as she turned and realized Evan had come into the yard and was watching them, just as she'd asked him to do.

Brent picked up the bottle of lube and moved behind

her. A moment later, he tossed the bottle on the grass, then his slick fingers stroked between her cheeks. His fingertip stroked her opening, then glided slowly inside her. She tightened around his invading finger, then released. Another finger slid inside and he stroked her. His thumb stretched around and found her slick vagina. As his fingers glided inside her back opening, his thumb stroked her slick passage and occasionally skimmed across her clit, sending electric tingles through her. He added another finger and moved all three inside her, stretching her gently.

"Oh, Brent. I'm so ready. I want your cock inside me. Let me feel it stretch me."

"Okay, baby, whatever you say."

His cockhead stroked between her cheeks, then pushed against her opening. She tensed, then forced herself to relax as he pressed against her. The tip slid in slowly, stretching her wide. She pushed with internal muscles, to open for him. Slowly, he moved inside her.

God, Brent was giving her just what she wanted. Filling her from the back with his cock. His cockhead was now fully inside and he stopped.

"You okay, baby?"

She nodded, then drew in a deep breath. She felt stretched beyond belief, his big member squeezed by her tight muscles. But she loved the feel of him inside her.

"I want more," she said.

He kissed her neck, then pressed forward, gliding his long shaft into her. Gently. Slowly. Until, finally, he filled her all the way.

"Fuck, that is the sexiest thing I've ever seen," Evan said behind her.

Brent wrapped his arms around her waist, and his body conformed to hers. He nuzzled her neck.

"Is this what you wanted?" he murmured.

"Oh, yes." She drew in a deep breath again. She ached with the feel of his big cock settled inside her, but it was a good ache. It triggered a longing for more. And that more was Evan.

"Now, I'd like us to sit down," she said.

Brent drew her back, his arms around her waist holding her tight to his body, then turned and settled on the bench, with her on his lap.

She glanced at Evan, who stood watching as Brent's lips caressed the base of her throat, sending tingles rippling through her. Brent cupped his hands over her breasts protectively and squeezed, but then he glided his palms underneath and lifted.

"Evan, join us."

Evan stared at Crystal and Brent in front of him. Brent held up Crystal's breasts as if offering them. Evan's cock throbbed with the need to be inside Crystal's hot body, but the change in Brent was throwing him a little off balance.

"Uh . . . sure." He shed his bathing suit and Crystal's gaze dropped to his erection, which throbbed with need.

He walked toward them, longing to touch her round breasts. To taste her luscious nipples. He leaned down and captured one in his mouth, conscious of his chin brushing against Brent's hand. Her nipple hardened in his mouth and he teased it with the tip of his tongue, then he sucked it inside, making her moan. He switched to the other and tortured her the same way. Then he stood up.

She wrapped her hand around his cock and admired it.

"Mmm. You and Brent both have the most gorgeous cocks." She stroked her finger from base to tip. "What do you think, Brent?"

Evan became increasingly aware that Brent's face was very close to Crystal's and only inches from Evan's cock. Brent stared at Evan's cock and nodded.

Crystal pressed Evan's cock to her mouth and licked. "Mmm. Delicious." She swirled around the tip, then gazed at it lovingly.

Evan's cock twitched in her hand. He became intensely conscious of Brent staring at his cock as Crystal held it in her hand, admiring it.

Then Brent leaned forward and licked it. Evan stiffened, and jagged sensations rocked through him. He couldn't tell if it was pleasure or pain.

What the fuck was going on?


The look of shock on Evan's face almost matched the shock Brent felt at his own action. God, with his aching cock deep in Crystal's ass . . . and watching Evan suck her tits . . . God, he could barely think straight with the rage of hormones surging through him.

But with that huge, purple-headed cock staring him in the face, Brent simply couldn't help himself.

Crystal pressed Evan's cockhead to her lips. Brent watched as it disappeared into her mouth. His cock twitched inside her.

He realized that letting go of his hesitation and doing what felt right was the best decision he could make. It was the only way to figure out what it was he really wanted. He'd have to explore these urges before he could work out the complicated relationship among the three of them. It was a help that Crystal was being wild and sexy. Wanting forbidden experiences. God, she wanted his best friend to fuck her while he fucked her ass. That was kinky and hot and turned him on immensely.

Now he just had to hope that he didn't totally freak out Evan.

Crystal released Evan's cockhead, then with a big smile offered it to Brent again.

Brent stared at the bulbous head in front of him, a clear drop oozing from the tip. Without allowing thoughts to cloud his judgment, he leaned forward and swallowed the bulbous head into his mouth. It was weird and crazy to be doing this, but somehow it felt right, too. He squeezed Evan's cockhead, then sucked, just as Crystal did to Brent when she pleasured him.

Evan's eyes widened, but then they closed as Brent continued to suck. Then he ran his tongue around the tip, tasting the salty precum. Finally, Brent released him. Evan's gaze shot to Brent's.

"Ah, man, this is intense." Evan's voice sounded shaky.

"I know, but what the hell?" Brent said. "Who cares

what anyone else would think about it? Let's just leave any of that crap out of this."

"What we do here is just between us," Crystal said. "No judgment. Just pleasure."

Brent reached for Evan's cock again and sucked it into his mouth, then drew it deep inside. The feel of a long, hard shaft in his mouth was different and . . . exciting. He sucked and stroked. Slowly, Evan began to move forward and back, filling Brent's mouth with more of his cock, then less, then surged forward with more again.

Crystal, whose face was extremely close to the action, watched them with wide eyes. Brent felt her fingers brush against his balls, and he realized she was stroking her wet opening, with occasional brushes against him.

Brent drew Evan from his mouth and pressed the wet cock to Crystal's mouth. She opened wide and took him deep inside.

"We've got her so hot," Brent said, "that she's stroking her pussy." He felt her fingers brush him again. "And my balls."

"Really?" Evan's voice sounded strained and excited. "Well, she's certainly sucking my cock with gusto."

Brent stroked down Crystal's belly, then glided his fingers inside her pussy along with hers. "Now I'm stroking her pussy, too."

When he moved to her clit and teased it with his slick fingertip, she groaned around Evan's big cock. With her hot passage squeezing him tightly, Brent's own cock throbbed with the need to explode inside her ass.

She pulled Evan's cock from her mouth and pushed it to Brent. He swallowed it and sucked hard.

"This is *such* a turn-on. I can't believe we're doing this, but it feels *incredible*," Crystal said.

Evan pulled back, his cock dropping from Brent's mouth, and he leaned over and captured her lips. After his tongue swept deep into her mouth, Evan drew away and began to move toward Brent's mouth, but suddenly he stopped.

Evan's uncertain gaze caught Brent's. Brent nodded and Evan swooped forward and pressed his lips to Brent's. The warm, masculine lips against his felt strange, but with the electric sexuality charging the air, Brent welcomed them. Opened to them. Evan's tongue glided into his mouth, and Brent answered with a stroke from his own. Their tongues tangled and swayed together as their lips moved on each other.

"Oh, God, you're . . . ," Crystal moaned, her pelvis rocking on his cock. She brushed aside his fingers, which had gone lax on her clit, and stroked herself. "You're so fucking sexy."

Spurred on by her excitement, Brent grasped Evan's face and deepened the kiss.

"Oh, yes." Crystal sucked in air, then moaned.

Evan drew back and nuzzled Crystal's neck as Brent watched pleasure wash across her features. At her orgasm, Brent nearly lost it. But he held on, forcing his body to hold back his intense need to release.

Her moans faded, and she opened her eyes.

"God, Evan, I want you inside me, too."

Evan knelt in front of her and pressed his cockhead to her opening, then glided forward, impaling her with one sure stroke. She grasped his shoulders and held him tight to her body.

"This is what I want." Emotion laced her words. "For all three of us to be together like this. For all three of us to find pleasure together."

She kissed Evan, then turned to find Brent's lips. His groin ached at the feel of her soft, feminine lips. He could taste the same vodka lemonade on her lips that he had on Evan's.

Sharing. They were all truly sharing now. Tastes, textures. Bodies. The intense sensuality . . . and freedom . . . of the situation overwhelmed him.

Evan's lips swept over Brent's again and their tongues entwined for a second, then Brent's mouth returned to Crystal's.

Brent wrapped his hand around her jaw and nuzzled her temple while his other hand found her breast. His thumb toyed with her rigid, protruding nipple.

"Crystal, this is so fucking hot," Brent murmured. "If I don't fuck you soon, I think I'll die."

She giggled, her lips parting from Evan's. With her flushed face and her eyes glistening with unbridled passion, she had never looked more beautiful.

"God, yes. Please fuck me. Both of you."

Evan groaned and thrust forward, driving her body deeper onto Brent's cock. Evan drew away and drove forward again. Crystal murmured deep in her throat.

As Evan thrust, Brent felt as though Evan were fucking

him as well as Crystal. And as Brent's cock filled Crystal, he felt as if he were fucking Evan, too. Because together, as they moved inside Crystal, they were pleasuring each other. This was what a threesome should be, he realized. Three lovers together in the truest sense. Brent turned Crystal's head so he could kiss her. As soon as their lips joined, Evan pressed his mouth to theirs, too. Crystal flicked her tongue between them, and soon all three of their tongues danced between their mouths.

Then Crystal gasped and drew away. "Oh, God, I'm . . ." She gasped again. "You're both making me . . ." She moaned. "Come."

Evan groaned, and Brent could see his face contort as he climaxed. Brent's cock swelled, then he exploded inside her hot body with enough force to catapult him to the moon. He clung to Crystal, reveling in her soft body against him as her tight passage squeezed his cock to intense pleasure as he shot to the stars.


An hour later, Brent headed to the beach for a walk, his hair still damp from his shower. The euphoria of the intimate encounter among the three of them had begun to fade. The soft sound of the water caressing the shore helped to calm his rising anxiety, but only a fraction.

What the hell had he done? How had he allowed himself to get so carried away? The memory of Evan's mouth on his, their tongues tangling, sent a quiver through him, which was disconcerting. Even more disturbing was the memory of Evan's cock in his mouth. He'd enjoyed it at the time, caught up in the passionate spell among the three of them, but now . . .

Damn it, he was turned on by women, not men. How the hell could he enjoy touching Evan? And sucking his cock, for God's sake?

"Hey, Brent. Wait up."

Brent glanced around to see Evan running along the beach toward him. Damn it, guilt surged through him. How had he allowed things to go so far without having talked to Evan first? He stopped walking and waited for his friend to catch up.

"You look as freaked out as I feel," Evan said. "I think maybe you and I need to talk."

# Twenty-one

Crystal watched through the patio door as Brent walked past the pool toward the house. Her stomach tilted at his serious expression. She stepped back as he opened the patio door.

"Where's Evan?" she asked.

"He . . . needs some time to himself." He stepped inside. "Crystal, we need to talk."

Butterflies swirled in her stomach. Those words were never good.

"What is it?" she asked.

"Let's go sit down." Brent pressed his hand to her lower back and guided her to the living room.

Her insides twisted. Definitely not good.

She sat on the couch and he sat beside her, but slanting at an angle to face her, his hands folded between his knees as he leaned toward her.

"I think maybe you should make your choice between Evan and me."

Her chest compressed. "You want me to decide now?" Oh, God, she couldn't do that. She simply couldn't. She loved them both.

"I think it's a good idea."

She shook her head. "But I'm just . . . not ready."

They had another week here. She should at least be able to enjoy their unconventional relationship for another week.

"I know. But it's not going to get any easier."

She drew in a deep breath to calm her quivering insides, but it didn't help much. "Why now?" She knew they'd both been a bit thrown off by this afternoon's sexual escapade, but she thought they just needed time to get used to the idea. "Is it because of this afternoon? Because that was so great, it . . ."

At the flicker of pain in Brent's eyes, she paused.

She rested her hand on his arm. "Brent?"

He shook his head. "We can't do that again."

"But why? It was so sexy and I know we all enjoyed it."

"Maybe too much," Brent muttered between clenched teeth.

She tipped her head. "What do you mean?"

He sighed. "I mean Evan wasn't comfortable with what happened."

"Oh." She knew Evan had liked the idea of a threesome, but when the men had started touching . . . kissing . . . He'd seemed to be into it at the time, but clearly he had second thoughts now. "But you're okay with it, aren't you? Maybe we just need to give Evan a little time."

Brent sighed. "Okay, here's the problem. I . . ." His hands clenched. "Damn it."

She squeezed his arm. "Just tell me," she said softly.

"I . . ." He gazed at her, searching for understanding in her eyes. "I *want* it to happen again."

Confusion swirled through her. "Well, that's good, isn't it?"

"No."

The sharpness of his voice startled her. She shook her head, gazing at him in confusion.

"The problem is," he repeated in a tight, controlled voice, "I want it *too* much."

Understanding dawned. "You're saying that . . . you're attracted to Evan. And he's not comfortable with that."

"*I'm* not comfortable with it, either."

"But, what we all shared this afternoon was . . . magical."

"Maybe. Evan might disagree."

"No. He was enjoying it. I'm sure of it."

"What we did today has thrown everything out of kilter. Evan is freaked out, and . . . well, I've been struggling with it for a while now."

She gazed at his face. "How long . . . have you known? About your feelings for Evan?"

"They're not feelings, they're . . ." His balled hands clenched tighter. "Fuck, I don't know what they are."

"Okay, let's think about this. You're saying you are sexually attracted to him, right?"

He nodded reluctantly, a sour expression on his face.

"Did you talk to him about it?" She assumed that was what happened out on the beach and why Brent had come back so upset. And why Evan wasn't here now.

"Yeah. You noticed he didn't come back with me."

"Okay, so let me ask you this. If Evan *was* okay with this, how would you feel?"

His gaze darted to hers.

*What am I thinking, asking a guy about his feelings?*

"What I'm asking is," she continued, "if Evan were okay with this, would you be, too?"

His lips compressed.

"Because, you know," she continued, "if you were both okay with it, it would strengthen what we all have together. Maybe we could even find a way to be together somehow—all three of us—in the long term." She took his hand. "Just think of it. It wouldn't be just about each of you being with me. It would be about all three of us."

She wanted to say loving one another, but Brent's attitude was too fragile right now. She had to take it slowly. To help him—to help both of them—understand that these feelings were a wonderful thing.

As long as Evan returned them.

"That's great conjecture, but I don't see Evan coming on board."

"Maybe I can talk to him."


"Hey there."

Evan glanced around at the sound of Crystal's voice.

"May I join you?" she asked.

He nodded and she sat on the sand beside him, placing a small, soft-sided cooler next to her.

"I brought you some cold lemonade." She unzipped the blue padded bag and opened it. "I brought some water, too."

He reached in and pulled out a plastic bottle of pink lemonade, single-serving size, then unscrewed the cap and took a sip of the icy liquid. "Thanks."

She rested her arms on her bent knees and gazed out over the ocean. "Brent told me about your talk. I thought I'd come find you and see how you're doing."

He sighed. "I'm a little confused. It's not every day you find out your best friend of twenty years has the hots for you."

"I know. It must have thrown you off a lot." She gazed at him, her eyes full of concern. "But, you know, nothing has really changed."

He gazed at her, his eyebrows raised. "Nothing?"

She smiled. "Okay, so there's some physical stuff, but . . . it was good." Her eyes glittered with heat. "*Really* good."

God, he remembered how much it had turned her on when she'd watched him and Brent touching . . . kissing. And Evan had enjoyed it at the time. A lot.

He shook his head. It was just so confusing.

The feel of Brent's tongue gliding into his mouth, firm and hard, not at all like the gentle nuzzling of Crystal's tongue.

Fuck! He grabbed Crystal's shoulders and captured

her mouth, devouring it, driving his tongue deep into her warmth. She was so soft. And feminine.

He drew back and gazed at her sweet face.

She stroked his cheek. "The fact that you enjoy being with Brent doesn't make you less manly. And it doesn't change how I feel about you." Her lips turned up in an impish grin. "Except for the fact that it makes you way more sexy."

He laughed, despite his turmoil.

"You know, he'd do anything to keep your friendship intact," she said.

Evan sat back and scooped up a handful of warm sand, then let the granules drizzle from his fingers.

"When he came back to the villa, he suggested I make my choice now," she continued. "He was sure you wouldn't want to continue with our threesomes and he was worried about putting a continued strain on your friendship." She gazed out over the ocean. "The problem is, even if I were to choose now, it wouldn't solve this problem. The relationship between you and Brent will continue to be strained. In fact, if we can't figure something out, it could be the end of your friendship."

Evan nodded. "It would give us an excuse not to see each other anymore. Because one of us was dumped."

Her soft hand covered his. "You don't really want to lose Brent as your friend, do you?"

Evan's chest tightened. He and Brent had been friends a long time. They'd always been there for each other. The thought of never seeing him again, of not having his best friend to lean on when things got tough, made him miserable. And losing Crystal, if it came to that, would be the hardest thing that ever happened to Evan. Losing Brent, *too,* would be devastating.

"No, I don't," he said.

"Okay, let me ask you something." She snuggled close to him, her warm skin delightfully soft against his. "When we were all together, all of us enjoying each other, it was really hot."

"That's not a question."

"I know. It's just that it looked like you were enjoying what was happening. If you did, is it really so bad that you and Brent enjoy each other in that way?"

He sucked in a deep breath and raised his hand to stroke his stubbly jaw. It felt so different from the smooth flesh of Crystal's soft face. More like what he'd feel if he touched Brent.

And the thought of touching Brent . . . although confusing him . . . also appealed to him on some level.

"No, I guess not. It's just . . . strange. I don't know how to act around him."

"What if it was some other guy? Not Brent. Would it still be strange?"

"I don't understand." He raised an eyebrow. "Are you suggesting that I might want sex with another guy?"

"Well, I just mean . . . you know how sexy you found it when Sarah and I did it."

The images that comment triggered sent a jolt of adrenaline through him. "Fuck, yeah."

"Well, I found it a little strange with Sarah at first, but then"—she shrugged—"I realized it was just sex. And you and Brent shared Sarah, but with no emotional attachments, so you could just enjoy it."

"Are you suggesting I get it on with Sarah's boyfriend?"

"Well, not exactly. I'm wondering if . . . well, if all five of us were to interact, then maybe it would help you and Brent relax a bit."

He stared at her. "Woman, your idea of relaxing is a strange one."

"I just mean Sarah and Kade have a relaxed attitude about sex. No judgments. Maybe with them, we could just go with the flow and become more comfortable with our sexual dynamic."

He wrapped his arms around his knees and stared across the ocean at the bright blue sky. Crystal wanted them to work this out. And Evan wanted to continue his friendship with Brent. Evan had told Crystal that if she chose him, he'd be happy to have Brent join them in the bedroom for threesomes.

And that thought appealed to him greatly.

In fact, the memory of this afternoon—of touching and being touched by Brent—turned him on immensely. He'd do anything to get past this knot of indecision and move forward. He really wanted to keep his friendship intact, and maybe Crystal's idea of being around people with open minds about sex would help.

"Evan, if the idea makes you uncomfortable, then we can just drop it."

He turned and gazed at her.

"No, I think it's worth a try."

Evan walked with Crystal and Brent along the stone path to the villa where Sarah and Kade were staying.

Crystal paused at the front door and turned toward them. "Are you two sure you're okay with this?"

Brent glanced at Evan.

"Yeah. Let's do it." Even though Evan's stomach fluttered, he'd actually been looking forward to it. At least, the idea of being with Sarah again. And watching Crystal and Sarah interact. And even the thought of Crystal taking on that huge cock this Kade guy sported.

Crystal knocked. A few moments later, Sarah opened the door, stunning in thigh-high black boots and a tight red vinyl dress with a zipper down the front and a plunging neckline, her generous breasts straining at the fabric.

Evan's cock twitched at the thought that he'd soon see them naked again.

Sarah smiled as she closed the door behind them. "You really are a lucky woman, Crystal." Her hungry gaze wandered up and down Evan's body, making his cock harden, then shifted to Brent. "To have two such gorgeous hunks."

Her lips curled in a sexy smile, then she turned and led them into the house. Damn, the sway of her hips as she walked would turn any man's cock into a pillar of stone.

Brent followed Sarah and Crystal into the living room, Evan trailing behind them. Brent couldn't believe Evan had agreed to this. Whatever Crystal had said to him had worked wonders.

Brent was both excited and uncertain about their impending sexual adventure, but he felt optimistic that it would help him and Evan move forward. And a part of him found the whole idea to be an extreme turn-on. He was a little nervous about interacting with this other man, but he was curious at the same time. It helped knowing that Sarah and Kade were so open about sex.

Then there was Crystal. He knew she was curious about being with a guy with such a big cock, and Brent found the idea of her sucking that big member while he watched intensely erotic. As for the guy fucking Crystal, arousal at the thought warred with jealousy, but arousal was definitely winning.

"So how are you two feeling about this evening?" Sarah asked. "A little uncertain?"

Brent caught Evan's eye, then they both stared at Sarah again.

"It is a little strange," Evan answered. He sat on the couch, and Brent sat in one of the easy chairs across from it.

She nodded. "Well, maybe a little wine will relax you."

As she walked toward the sideboard, Brent couldn't help but notice her sensational round ass, the shiny red fabric of her dress stretched tightly across it. Then his gaze shifted to her long, shapely legs encased in thigh-high, black patent-leather boots, which left only a few inches of naked flesh visible below the hem of her dress. Which was sexy as hell.

She poured four glasses of red wine. Crystal picked up two and handed one to Brent. Sarah handed another to Evan.

"To a wonderful evening." Sarah held her glass forward and everyone clinked their glasses to hers. She tipped hers back, finishing half the contents.

Brent tipped his back, finishing it in one gulp. He savored the heat washing down his throat.

"So where's the other member of our little party?" Brent asked.

"Well, Kade's *tied up* at the moment." She smiled.

"I take it you don't mean he's busy," Evan said.

"Busy? There's no way Kade would let something else interfere with this evening." She refilled the men's empty wineglasses, then topped up Crystal's and hers. "We thought a little bondage might make it more exciting. And put you more at ease."

"At ease?" Brent asked.

"Yes. If the new male is . . . on a leash, shall we say."

"What about you?" Evan asked. "Are you going to be tied up, too?"

Sarah's smile turned devilish. "Me? No. In fact, I plan to be in charge." With that, she grabbed the tag of the zipper on the front of her dress and tugged it down.

Brent's gaze darted to her breasts, freed from the tight fabric. She dropped the dress to the ground and stood before them in a shiny black vinyl corset and thong. Her legs looked sensational augmented by the thigh-high boots with five-inch steel stiletto heels.

"So how about it? Will you do as I command?" Sarah asked.

"Uh . . . sure," Brent answered.

"Absolutely." Evan grinned.

"The correct answer is, 'Yes, Mistress.'" Sarah turned to Crystal. "And what about you?"

"Yes, Mistress," Crystal answered, her eyes wide.

"Good, now follow me." Sarah turned around, flashing an eyeful of delightfully round ass, which swayed as she walked down the stairs, then along a hall. She turned right and opened a door.

Brent peered in as he followed the others inside. Standing against the wall at the other end of the room stood a naked man. His wrists were chained together, and his hands rested over his groin. A blindfold covered his eyes. God damn, the man bulged with muscles. Brent wasn't fully comfortable with viewing a man as a potential sexual partner, but this guy screamed masculine appeal. No one could deny how fucking totally sexy this guy was.

He glanced toward Crystal, and his heart thundered at the look of fascination in her eyes as she stared at the guy.

# Twenty-two

Crystal couldn't tear her gaze from Kade. He was stunning standing there, his bulging muscles glistening in the soft light of the room. His hands covered his cock, but she remembered its extreme length and girth when he was aroused, and she longed to wrap her hands around his erection and stroke it right now. To lick the tip, then take it in her mouth.

"Kade, I've brought some friends. Are you ready to serve them?"

"Yes, Mistress."

Crystal's insides heated as she thought about how Kade would *serve* her.

"Good. Now, Brent and Evan, take off your shirts," Sarah commanded.

Crystal watched as Evan and Brent unfastened the buttons of their shirts, then shed them.

"Crystal, chain them to the wall."

For the first time, Crystal noticed cuffs dangling from

chains attached to the wall. She stepped toward Evan and fastened his wrists with one pair of cuffs, then did the same to Brent. The fiery glow in Evan's eyes told her that even though he was uncertain about all this, he was turned on by the situation.

"Take off their pants."

Crystal unfastened Brent's belt, then the button on his jeans. A bulge swelled beneath the fabric. She unfastened the zipper, then eased his jeans down his legs to his feet. Next, she grasped the waistband of his boxers and drew them downward. As his naked cock bounced free, she wanted to wrap her hands around it and stroke. To suck the tip into her mouth. But she eased the pants and boxers from his feet and pushed them aside, then moved to Evan. She divested him of his pants and boxers, too, nearly licking his cock as it bobbed in front of her but restraining herself.

"Now remove Kade's blindfold."

Crystal walked across the room toward Kade, feeling the heat inside her ramp up as she drew closer. She reached behind his head and unfastened the loose knot holding the blindfold in place, then drew away the strip of fabric. His eyes glimmered as he stared at her. A half smile flashed across his face, then disappeared as he composed his features into the bland expression of a good submissive.

"Come here, Crystal," Sarah commanded.

Crystal returned to the center of the room, and Sarah moved behind her. She could feel the pull of her dress zipper as Sarah unfastened it. She drew it down Crystal's shoulders and it fell to her waist. Sarah eased it over Crystal's hips and the garment fell to the floor.

It felt so sexy being stripped in front of three men, their gazes locked on her.

"Very nice. Now kick off your shoes."

Crystal stepped out of her white heels and stood in front of them in only her frilly pink bra and panties, which Sarah had suggested she wear, with no stockings. Simple and feminine. A sharp contrast to the wicked Domme outfit worn by Sarah.

Sarah's hands stroked around Crystal's ribs, then glided over her breasts. Her nipples puckered at the sensation. Sarah pushed her fingertips under the lace cups and stroked the hard nubs, to the total fascination of all three men. They watched the lacy fabric move over Sarah's busy fingers. Sarah dragged one of her hands down Crystal's ribs and over her stomach, then lingered over her navel, the fingertips brushing the top of her panties. The men's tongues almost hung out as they watched.

Then Sarah's fingers slipped under the elastic of the panties and lowered. Crystal sucked in a breath at the feel of Sarah's fingers stroking her slit.

"Kade, come over here."

Kade walked toward them, his hands continuing to rest on his lovely cock, but Crystal could see the tip rising above his wrists.

Sarah stepped from behind Crystal and took a key from between her breasts, then unfastened Kade's cuffs.

"You remember what I told you to do right now, don't you?"

"Yes, Mistress." Kade locked gazes with Crystal, and she felt her vagina weep with need. But then he walked toward Evan. Kade knelt in front of him.

Kade's hands moved away from his groin, and Crystal drank in the sight of his huge cock, until he wrapped his hand around Evan's erection.

Evan's body stiffened.

Sarah raised an eyebrow. "Are you open to new experiences?"

"Yeah. Sure." But Evan glanced at Crystal uncertainly. She smiled at him encouragingly.

The thought of Kade touching Evan . . . of him stroking Evan's cock . . . turned her on immensely.

"To be fair, if you allow us to explore this particular experience"—Sarah smiled wickedly—"then I'll do anything you want me to do to Crystal."

At that, she crouched and pulled Crystal's panties down her thighs, then glided her hand between Crystal's legs and stroked over her naked folds. Crystal moaned a little, then Sarah drew her hand away.

"What do you say?"

Evan's cock had lengthened at the sight of Sarah stroking Crystal. He grinned. "I'm thinking I'd like to see a little more action before I decide."

"Crystal, turn around and lean over," Sarah commanded.

Evan watched as Crystal kicked off her panties, but his thoughts kept flicking back to the image of the gigantic dick on Kade. All that muscle, good looks, and a cock big enough to make any woman swoon.

Crystal turned around and bent over at the waist, revealing her naked pussy. Evan's heart thundered as Sarah stroked over her slick folds, then separated them a little.

"I'll lick her here."

Oh, God.

"Okay," Evan said, his gaze glued to Sarah's hands on Crystal's wet flesh.

Kade's hand encircled Evan's cock and he stroked. Evan's spine stiffened at the unaccustomed intimacy, but then Sarah leaned down and licked Crystal's pussy. Then Sarah's mouth moved more firmly onto her slick opening. Watching Sarah's mouth moving against Crystal's glistening pussy, and the feel of the firm hand stroking his cock up and down, sent Evan's hormones humming.

Kade reached out with his other hand and grasped Brent's cock, then began stroking him, too. Evan relaxed a little. The firm stroking, the sight of Sarah leaning down and licking Crystal's sweet little pussy, sent blood flooding through his groin. At the feel of a hot mouth surrounding his cock, he groaned. The man was sucking his cock. And, God, it felt incredible.

In front of him, Sarah pushed a finger into Crystal and she moaned. Evan's cock slid deep into Kade's hot, wet mouth, all the way to the base, then Kade sucked and squeezed.

Evan lost it. His balls tightened and he gushed into the guy's throat.

As soon as he'd finished ejaculating, Kade released him, then crouched in front of Brent. It was strange and yet a real turn-on watching Kade take Brent into his mouth and suck him deep. Across the room, Sarah's mouth continued moving on Crystal's intimate flesh, and Evan realized Crystal was gazing into a big mirror on the wall, watching Kade suck Brent. Her face was flushed and she looked close to orgasm.

Brent was watching Crystal as Kade bobbed up and down on his cock. Sarah slid another finger into Crystal and began gliding them in and out while she continued to lick her. When Crystal began to moan again, Brent groaned and arched forward. Both of them came to orgasm at the same time.

"Kade, bring me a stool," Sarah said.

Kade stood up and retrieved a stool from a corner of the room. He set it in front of Sarah.

"Now sit."

Kade sat on the stool, his enormous cock sticking straight up.

"Crystal, suck his lovely cock for me."

Crystal sank to her knees in front of Kade and wrapped her hands around that enormous dick. She began to stroke. Up and down. Then she leaned forward and wrapped her lips around the gigantic cockhead. Evan felt his cock stiffen again. Sarah knelt beside Crystal and wrapped her mouth around the side of the thick shaft, then glided up and down. Crystal dove downward until her mouth brushed Sarah's, then drew back up. Sarah followed her. Crystal slid off the end of the big cock, and Sarah did, too, then their lips met and the two women kissed, their mouths moving passionately together.

Evan's groin tightened as he watched the two women kiss. Man, they were so hot.

Crystal wrapped her lips around one side of Kade's shaft, and Sarah did the same on the other side, then they glided up and down in unison. Kade's hard cock twitched as their tongues and lips stimulated him. Crystal's fingers found his balls, stroking gently.

After several long moments of both of them licking and sucking him, Sarah brushed her long blonde hair from her face and stood up.

"He's going to be stubborn." She smiled. "Which is a good thing. Stand up, Crystal."

Crystal glided off the end of his wonderful cock and stood up.

"Take off her bra, Kade."

Crystal moved in front of Kade, presenting her back to him, and he unhooked her bra. She dropped the lacy item forward and released it. Both Brent and Evan stared at her breasts with longing, their cocks swelling with need. Kade wrapped his hands around her waist, then glided upward to cup her breasts. Her nipples peaked, pushing into his warm palms. He stroked them softly as he kissed along her spine, sending tingles dancing across her flesh.

"You have lovely breasts," Sarah said. "Kade, let Crystal sit on the stool."

Kade stood up and Crystal took his place. Sarah took one of Crystal's hard nipples into her mouth. The moist heat of her sent pleasure spiking through Crystal. Kade sank to his knees in front of her and pressed her knees wide, then he dipped his head forward. She moaned at the intense sensation of his tongue dragging over her wet slit.

Hot desire lanced through her and she arched forward, wanting more of Kade's mouth on her. He drew her folds apart and found her clit with his tongue. She clung to his head as he dabbed and teased.

Sarah sucked on her nipple and Crystal moaned. She leaned back and almost fell off the stool. Kade caught her and drew her forward. She gazed longingly at his rigid cock.

"Oh, God, I want you to fuck me." The need rippling through her echoed in her voice.

"Afraid not, hon," Sarah answered. "Not yet. Kade, go free Evan and Brent."

Kade stood up, his cock bouncing close to her face. She almost grabbed it, but he turned and walked to the wall, then unfastened the cuffs holding Brent and Evan prisoners.

"Now, gentlemen, we're going up to the master bedroom. Kade, carry Crystal."

Crystal stood up as Kade approached, then he leaned forward and pressed his shoulder to her stomach and wrapped his hand around her thighs. Next thing she knew, she was draped over his shoulder, her bare ass exposed for all to see as he carried her up the stairs, then down another hallway. Sarah opened the door to the bedroom and he flopped her on the bed.

"Crystal, there are three gorgeous cocks here. I want you to suck them all."

Crystal sat up and grabbed the closest cock. Brent's. She licked him, then wrapped her mouth around him and sucked. She bobbed up and down, then released him. Evan stepped up next. She sucked his long cock into her mouth and drew him deep, then teased him with her tongue as she moved. When he withdrew, Kade's cock pressed to her lips. She opened wide and swallowed his cockhead, then swirled her tongue over his tip.

He withdrew, then came Brent again, filling her mouth. Then Evan. Then Kade. Each pushed into her mouth in turn.

"God, you're all making me so hot," Sarah said. "I want you men to undress me."

Brent's cock slipped from Crystal's mouth and he joined the other two men standing beside Sarah. Crystal watched as Brent leaned over and unfastened the zipper on Sarah's boot while Kade unhooked her corset. Evan drew down her panties. More and more of Sarah's naked flesh became visible as Brent slipped off one boot and Evan unzipped the other one, then Kade peeled away the black leather corset. Evan slid off the second boot and tossed it aside, his gaze firmly focused on the soft blonde curls between her legs.

Sarah stood totally naked, her long blonde hair gleaming as it cascaded over her shoulders and down around her puckered nipples. She tossed it back, giving the men an eyeful of her lusciously full breasts. She stepped toward Crystal and pressed one of those breasts forward. Crystal took the hard nipple in her mouth and sucked. Sarah moaned and all three men groaned their appreciation. Crystal switched to the other nipple and sucked, while teasing the first damp nipple with her fingertips.

"Oh, God, I need someone to fuck me." Sarah slipped away from Crystal. "Kade, lie on the bed. I want to feel that big, thick cock in me while one of the others fucks me in the ass."

Kade sat on the bed about a foot from Crystal, then lay down. Sarah climbed on top of him, her knees on either side of his hips, and pressed his big erection to her opening. Slowly, she lowered herself onto him. Crystal's insides twitched as she wished it were her feeling that hard, heavenly shaft push into her.

Once Sarah had him fully inside, she lifted her ass. "There are condoms and lubricant on the bedside table. One of you get them and get inside me," she demanded.

Evan grabbed a packet, then ripped it open and rolled on the condom. Then he squeezed the clear gel onto his hands and slathered it over his cock. He pressed his cock to Sarah's round ass and slowly glided inside.

The three of them began to move. The movement of the bed beneath her and the moans of pleasure beside her sent Crystal's hormones spiraling out of control. She gazed at Brent, desperate longing oozing through her. He nodded with a smile and strode to her. She wrapped her hand around his cock and swallowed him whole, then sucked deeply.

He groaned, then grabbed her hands. She released his cock as he drew her to her feet. His lips found hers and he kissed her passionately, sending her heart pounding. He eased her to the carpeted floor, then prowled over her and pressed his cock against her slick opening. As he pushed inside, she wrapped her legs around him, then gasped as he drove deep.

God, he felt incredible inside her. He drew back and thrust deep again. He captured her lips, then continued to kiss her as he drove into her again and again. Tumultuous waves of pleasure rocked through her, rising higher and higher, until she was flung over the edge in an earthshattering orgasm, crying out in ecstasy.

"Hey, you guys kind of cheated there."

Crystal opened her eyes to see Sarah, Evan, and Kade all sitting on the side of the bed watching them.

"You're supposed to be following orders," Sarah said. "Now you'll have to be punished."

Brent stood up and took Crystal's hand and eased her to her feet as Kade rolled a condom over his gigantic cock. Sarah guided Crystal to the side of the bed, then tossed some pillows down and pressed her forward until she leaned against them, her ass exposed. Kade's enormous cock pressed against her, then pushed against her back opening.

Oh, God, he wasn't going to try going in there, was he?

Tingles danced through her, wondering what it would feel like to have his huge erection push inside her there.

He pulsed against her a few times, then shifted and pushed into her wet slit. He stretched her as he slowly eased inside. She grasped the bedding and clung to it as he pushed deeper inside her. She wanted to cry out at the sheer pleasure of his cock filling her so full.

Then he slipped away and Evan's cock glided inside. He slipped in easily, not filling her quite so full, but he spiraled and her breath caught.

Sarah lay down on the bed in front of her. "Brent, I want you to fuck me."

Brent walked to the other side of the bed, and Crystal could see that his cock had revived, probably from watching two hard cocks slip inside her. Evan withdrew and Kade pushed inside again. Brent put on a condom and climbed over Sarah, then pressed his cock to her opening. Crystal watched as Brent's cock disappeared inside her.

Kade, still embedded in her, wrapped his arms around Crystal's waist and eased her torso from the bed. Evan sat down and Kade slid his cock from her, then turned her around, her back to Evan. Evan drew her back and pressed his cock to her small puckered opening, then eased inside. She sucked in a breath as his hard cock filled her ass. Kade stood in front of her and pressed his cockhead to her wet slit. Then he drove inside. She gasped. His big cock filled her, stretching her delightfully. Evan's cock stretched her back opening.

Slowly, the two men moved inside her and she moaned. They filled her again and again. Thrusting deep. Filling her so full, she thought she'd burst. Her insides quivered and she could barely catch her breath as she clung to Kade's shoulders.

Pleasure erupted inside her and she catapulted to a

state of bliss. Kade and Evan groaned, and heat filled her insides, accelerating her rapture to dizzying heights. She cried out as the erotic wave of sensation blasted through her, erupting into blazing ecstasy.

Finally she gasped, then slumped between them.

# Twenty-three

Evan sipped his coffee as he leaned against the kitchen counter. He wasn't sure how he felt about anything anymore. The episode with the five of them had been hot and intense, and he was glad he'd taken part, but he still didn't know how he felt about his changing relationship with Brent. And he was keenly aware that Crystal still had to choose between them, and no matter which one of them she chose, it would adversely affect their friendship. It was all fine and good to think that they could continue fucking together, but that's all it would be. Fucking. He wanted more with Crystal. He wanted to be the man she spent her life with. Had children with. Grew old with. If she chose Brent, leaving Evan on the outside . . . Damn, he didn't know how to cope with that.

"Hey, how are you this morning?" Crystal walked into the kitchen, her skin glistening with dampness, her long wet hair tumbling around her face. The bikini she wore lifted her breasts and revealed a generous amount of round flesh.

Evan had woken up alone in bed this morning. When he'd walked into the kitchen, he'd seen Brent and Crystal romping in the pool.

She walked across the room and snuggled against his back, then kissed between his shoulder blades. "We didn't want to wake you. It was such a gorgeous day, we decided to go for a swim."

Evan turned around and took her in his arms, then found her mouth. Her soft lips—cold because of her swim—pressed against his made his body harden. He swept his tongue inside her mouth, needing to join with her.

"Mmm. I think someone's hungry." She smiled up at him.

"And not for food." He lifted her and set her on the counter, then pulled her tight to his body, her knees hugging his hips.

Desire flooded through him as his cock nestled in the cradle of her body, only two thin layers of fabric—his boxers and her flimsy bikini bottoms—providing a barrier between them. God, he wanted to feast on her swelling breasts, to pull aside the fabric blocking him and glide into her. To feel her body envelop him.

"Looks like you guys are starting without me." Brent grinned from the doorway.

Shit. Evan would love to have Crystal alone, to make love to her passionately, to show her how much he loved her.

Evan held Crystal's gaze. She stroked his cheek and

gazed back sympathetically, as if she knew what he was feeling. He drew back, missing the feel of her warm skin against his naked chest and the comfort of her heat embracing his cock.

"Don't stop because of me," Brent said. "If you like, I can just watch."

A part of Evan wanted to pull away. He longed to have her alone, without Brent present at all, but at least this gave him the opportunity to make love to her solo.

He pulled her to him and captured her lips, driving his tongue deep. Claiming her. When he released her, she sucked in a breath, then pulled him back again for another lip-grinding kiss. Her tongue dove into his mouth and he stroked it with his own, then they undulated together in a tumultuous dance of passion.

His heart thundered in his chest as he pulled her tighter against him, her soft breasts crushing against his chest. He found the clasp on the back of her bikini top and released it, then drew back and pulled it free from her body. Her dusky nipples puckered. He leaned down and captured one in his mouth, licking and stroking the hard nub with his tongue, then he sucked it hard. She gasped, her fingers coiling in his hair and pulling him tighter to her soft breast. He licked and nuzzled, then found the other nipple and sucked it deep.

"Oh, God, Evan." Her head lolled back against the kitchen cupboard behind her.

He smiled, loving the glow of desire lighting her features. He untied the sides of her bikini bottom and pulled the front down, exposing her delightful shaven pussy.

He wanted to taste her, to press his tongue into her wet opening and lick around and around, then nuzzle her little button until he brought her to orgasm. But his cock ached with the need to be inside her. As if sensing his indecision, she stroked his bulge, then her fingers slipped inside his boxers. At the feel of her soft hand grasping his raging hard cock, he groaned. She pressed it to her opening—God, it was so wet—and shimmied forward on the counter, causing his cockhead to slip in a little.

He couldn't stand it. He drove forward, impaling her with one thrust. She gasped and clung to him, grasping his shoulders.

"Oh, baby, you feel so good."

"You too," she murmured in his ear.

He drew back and drove forward again. She moaned, her face glowing with desire. For him.

He felt special, being inside her like this. Being loved by her.

He thrust again and again. His cock ached with the need to release. She squeezed him inside her body and he groaned.

He kissed her neck. "God, I love it when you do that."

She squeezed again and he groaned again.

She nuzzled his neck. "Make me come, Evan."

He tucked her legs around his waist and she tightened them around him, then he cupped her buttocks and pulled her tighter to his body, his cock driving deeper than ever.

"Oh, yes." Her soft murmur accelerated his desire.

He drew back and thrust again. Then again. Soon he

was driving into her like a jackhammer, filling her with his hard cock over and over. Faster and faster.

"Oh, yes." She whimpered. "Oh, God, yes."

She tightened around him, her fingernails digging into his back. He filled her again and again. His cock ached with need, then his balls tightened. She gasped and moaned.

"Are you close?" His need to release burned through him.

"Yes, I'm going to . . . ahhh . . ."

He watched her eyes glaze as he drove into her, then she moaned.

"Yes, now. I'm . . . ahhh . . . you're making me . . ." She wailed as she burst into orgasm.

His cock exploded inside her, and he groaned. She squeezed him, gasping at her own pleasure. He rode the wave, pounding into her, fueling their shared bliss.

Finally, her head dropped against his shoulder. He drove deep one more time, holding their bodies tight together. She murmured her approval against his neck, then nuzzled delicately with her lips. He turned his head and captured those delicate lips, savoring the feel of their softness against his own.

"Fuck, you two were hot."

At the sound of Brent's voice . . . the reminder that they were not alone . . . Evan glanced toward his friend. But he wasn't unhappy. He had made love to Crystal . . . felt special in her arms. The fact that Brent had been there, watching, had not interfered with that at all.

In fact, the sight of Brent standing there naked, his

discarded trunks on the floor beside his feet, his hand wrapped around his big erection, actually had Evan's cock twitching for more.

But this time, with all three of them.

Brent was so fucking turned on having watched Evan's cock drive into Crystal, his big shaft appearing and disappearing as it speared into her. Now Evan walked toward him, the heat in his gaze palpable. Evan dropped to his knees in front of Brent and brushed Brent's hand away from his cock. Brent groaned as Evan's strong hand gripped him, then began to stroke.

Heat jolted through him as Evan's lips wrapped around his cock and Evan took him deep inside. As his mouth moved up and down, heat blazed through Brent's groin.

"Oh, fuck, man, I'm too fucking close. If you don't stop—"

Too late.

Evan opened his throat to allow Brent's big cock to go deep. It was hard and solid, and he couldn't get enough of it. Then hot liquid gushed into his throat. He swallowed the salty semen, then swallowed again as it kept flooding into him.

Man, he never would have thought he'd ever be doing this with another guy, but it was so fucking hot. Especially with Brent. As soon as he'd seen Brent's huge erection, a result of watching Evan and Crystal fucking, Evan hadn't been able to help himself. He'd wanted to feel it. In his hand, in his mouth. In fact, he even wondered if . . . would he go further than that?

"Now you two are both depleted," Crystal said.

He stood up and glanced around to see her still sitting on the counter, her legs spread wide, revealing her glistening pussy.

"Maybe I should come and help you both out." She grabbed the edge of the counter, ready to push herself off.

"No, you stay there and relax," Brent said, a gleam in his eye. "Evan's already recovering, and I'd like to help him out."

Brent crouched in front of Evan and wrapped his hand around Evan's cock, still slick from Crystal's essence.

"Mmm. You smell of Crystal." Brent stroked, then leaned forward and licked Evan's cockhead. "You taste of her, too."

Evan moaned as Brent swallowed the tip of his cock, then glided forward, taking Evan's shaft deeper, then back, then forward again. Brent's tongue laved around Evan's shaft as he moved.

"You two are so sexy," Crystal said.

Evan glanced around to see her stroking her naked breast with one hand and dipping the fingers of her other hand into her wet pussy.

"You like watching us suck each other's cocks, sweetheart?" Brent asked, also turning to watch her but holding Evan's erection firmly in the solid grip of his hand.

"Oh, yeah." She dipped her fingers in deeper, then

withdrew them and glided them into her mouth. Then sucked.

Evan's cock twitched uncontrollably.

Brent glanced at Evan. "It's so fucking hot watching her get off on watching us."

"Yeah. It makes you wonder what else we might do that would turn her on even more." Evan didn't know why he'd said it, but something spurred him on. Some deep need to experience more with Brent.

Brent's eyebrow arched up and he smiled. Crystal's eyes glittered, lust blazing in their depths.

"Do you think . . . are you guys thinking of doing . . . more?" she asked.

Evan sent Brent a querying gaze. Brent shrugged, but his eyes lit up.

"I'm game if you are."

"I'll go grab some condoms." Evan shot off to the master bedroom and grabbed the condoms and a bottle of lubricant.

When he returned, Brent was kissing Crystal, who still sat on the counter. As soon as Evan stepped into the room, Brent released Crystal's mouth, then placed his hands on either side of her and leaned forward.

Evan ripped open one of the packets and rolled the condom on his hard cock, then he applied a generous amount of lubricant gel. He stepped behind Brent and stroked his hard ass, then pressed his cockhead between his cheeks.

"You ready?" Evan asked.

In answer, Brent pressed his ass back against Evan. Evan pushed his cockhead against Brent's anus, then eased forward, feeling the small opening widen, then stretch around him. He moved slowly, easing in a bit at a time. Crystal peered over his shoulder with intense interest.

Once he was fully inside, Brent's passage squeezing Evan's cock tightly, he stopped.

"God, this has my cock hard as a rock," Brent murmured.

"Well, buddy," Evan said, "you don't have to waste a boner like that. I'm sure Crystal wouldn't mind keeping it warm for you."

Crystal's heart pounded. This was the most exciting thing she'd ever experienced, and given the past week, that was saying a lot. Brent tucked one hand on her lower back and slid her forward. When his cockhead brushed her wet opening, she arched her pelvis toward him. Both men pushed forward, driving Brent's cock into her.

She sucked in a breath.

"Oh, God," Brent groaned. "Do it, Evan."

Both their bodies jerked forward, driving Brent deep into her. Evan moved forward and back in a steady rhythm, filling Brent, causing Brent to fill her. She tightened around him, quivering in pleasure at the feel of his cock stroking inside her. That pleasure pulsed through her, building. Filling her with joy as an orgasm tore through her. Brent groaned as she tightened around him, then Evan grunted.

Immediately, Brent erupted inside her, filling her with liquid heat.

She clung to Brent's shoulders, riding the wave of their shared bliss. Their movements slowed, and when they finally stopped, she slumped against Brent's chest, her head snuggled into the curve of his shoulder. Evan nuzzled her temple, then she lifted her head and their lips met.

As they kissed, Brent turned his head and brushed his lips to theirs. Crystal's heart soared with hope that maybe somehow they would find a way to keep this closeness between them.

Brent opened his eyes to the bright afternoon sunshine, Crystal snuggled in his arms. After their rousing love-making, the three of them had stretched out on the bed and napped.

This vacation had opened his eyes to some things. Like how important Evan was in his life and how devastated he would be to lose him. As a friend and now as a lover. At least, a shared lover with Crystal. A lot of questions had haunted him since he'd discovered his attraction to his friend, but he knew that Crystal was the love of his life. If Crystal had never shown up in his life, would he have eventually wound up in an exclusive relationship with Evan? Probably not. It was just that the closeness he and Evan shared, and the fact that they enjoyed intimacy together, meant they could have a deeper relationship with Crystal together. Not just two guys sharing her, but the two of them sharing intimacy together. It made their threesomes more fulfilling.

He glanced past Crystal's sweet, sleeping face on the pillow beside him to Evan, but Evan wasn't there. Brent sat up slowly, trying not to disturb Crystal. She sighed and rolled onto her back. Brent stood up and opened the door, then closed it quietly behind him. He walked down the hall to the kitchen, then peered inside. Evan stood by the window, staring out at the pool glistening in the sunlight outside.

"Hey, what's up?"

Evan shook his head. "This whole thing . . . it's not going to work."

"What do you mean?"

Evan turned around and met Brent's gaze. "This thing with the three of us. It can't keep going."

Brent leaned back against the counter. "Maybe it doesn't have to end."

"Yeah, right. We'll be going back soon. Crystal's going to choose between us, and then . . ." His hands balled into fists. "We'll be back to life as normal. We aren't going to keep hooking up like this."

"There's no reason we have to end this. Even back home we could—"

"Look, I'm not stupid." Evan crossed his arms over his chest. "I know Crystal is going to choose you."

"You know she loves you."

"Yeah, and she loves you, too. Let's face it, if she loves us both the same—and that's a big if—then she's going to pick you. It's the only thing that makes sense. She already agreed to marry you. For her to pick me, she'd have to love me a whole lot more than you, which doesn't even make sense." He sighed. "When you love someone, you just love them. Heart and soul." He shrugged. "So the way I see it, she either loves us both the same or, more likely, she loves you and thinks of me as a really close friend. One she likes having sex with." He stared at Brent. "Come on, can you truthfully tell me you believe she might pick me over you?"

Brent stared at Evan. There was nothing he could say to make this better.

"Fuck, sorry. I know you want her to pick you," Evan said.

"Look, if she does pick me, we can still keep this going. It can be the three of us. Together."

"Yeah, like I want to be the odd man out. Looking at the two of you from outside."

"But you won't be—"

He scowled. "Of course I will be. You two will get married. Have kids. I'll be a part of it, sure. Uncle Evan to the kids. The best friend who's always there helping out. But as I said, I'll be looking in from outside." He slammed his fist against the counter in frustration. "I can't fucking do that. I love her. I want her to be my wife. To have my kids."

His anguished words tore at Brent's heart. He knew exactly what Evan meant.

Evan turned and faced Brent. "Fuck, sorry, man. I just . . ." His hands clenched at his sides. "Look, it'll be better for everyone if I just pull out. I have a chance at a job in New York. I'll just move on, give us all some distance. Then you two can find happiness without me hanging around making you feel guilty."

Brent's stomach clenched at his friend's words. "Damn it, Evan. I don't want you to move across the country. I don't want you to move anywhere. There's got to be a way to work this out."

"Man, if Crystal hadn't come into the picture . . . if we'd each found a woman of our own to love . . . then maybe our friendship could have lasted a lifetime. But once we both fell in love with the same woman . . ." He shrugged. "That's a recipe for disaster. The most important thing is that you and Crystal did fall in love, and you deserve that happiness. You can't let a friendship get in the way of that." His jaw tightened. "I wouldn't."

"Damn it, Evan, we just have to give this a chance. I really think there's an alternative."


Crystal stood outside the kitchen, listening. She'd heard most of the conversation between Brent and Evan. That Evan knew she'd pick Brent, and he was right. She did love both of them, so the only reasonable choice was Brent, the man she'd already agreed to marry.

Her heart ached at how Evan had talked about being on the outside looking in. Of course it would feel that way to him. She had begun to believe that the three of them could work out an arrangement to keep going the way they were, but how could they when it would just make Evan feel even more alone?

*If Crystal hadn't come into the picture . . . if we'd each found a woman of our own to love . . . then maybe our friendship could have lasted a lifetime.*

Damn. Now Evan was talking about moving to New York. Tears spilled from her eyes. She couldn't be responsible for breaking up their friendship. She dodged to the patio doors off the dining room and flew into the backyard.


Evan stopped midsentence at the sound of the patio doors in the other room opening. "Is that Crystal?"

He and Brent glanced out the window in time to see Crystal scurry across the backyard and disappear past the bushes.

"You think she heard us?" Evan asked.

"I'm sure of it."

"We'd better go after her." Evan started toward the door, but Brent grasped his arm.

"Yes, we should. But not yet. There's something I need to say first."

# Twenty-four

Crystal hurried across the backyard, the place where she and Brent and Evan had all discovered how close they really could be, and continued down the stone steps, then out the back gate to the beach.

Her heart ached as she wandered along the edge of the water. Would Evan really move to New York? That was across a continent. If he did that, she'd probably never see him again. And the friendship between him and Brent would definitely be over.

She wandered aimlessly for a while, sadness swirling through her, scattering her thoughts. She couldn't think straight. She felt overwhelmed and disheartened. Maybe talking to Sarah would help. Maybe Sarah would have some brilliant suggestion.

She turned back toward the villas and hurried along the beach. Disappointment seeped through her when she reached the lounge chairs and found Sara wasn't in her usual place.

Sarah had told Crystal that if she wasn't on the beach in the afternoons, she was usually tanning in the backyard, so Crystal headed toward the fence behind Sarah's yard.

She opened the combination lock, then stepped through the gate and pulled it closed behind her. She walked up the stone steps, along the path leading through the exotic plants toward the villa, and then stepped out of the dense foliage to where the yard opened up and she could see the pool. She continued past the pool house and glanced around—then stopped.

Sarah was nowhere to be seen, but Kade . . . Her insides quivered. Kade stood stark naked—all muscular six feet three of him—with water running over his sculpted body, which glistened in the sunlight. She licked her lips as she watched him in the outdoor shower. He was glorious and masculine and sexy, especially with his huge cock hanging free.

But he wasn't Brent or Evan.

He glanced up and smiled. "Crystal. What a delightful surprise." His smile faded as he watched her standing there. "Is something wrong?"

"I . . ." Oh, God, she was going to lose it. Her eyes started to water and she tried to stifle a sob, then she stepped under the water and into his arms.

He gathered her close and held her against his body. Big, strong, muscular . . . and comforting. She shivered in his arms as he held her. Not from cold, but from the intense emotions tumbling through her.

Then she felt a prickle along her spine, and she knew

she was not alone here with Kade. She glanced up to see Brent and Evan standing several yards away.

"Aren't two men enough for you?" Brent asked, his eyebrows raised.

Crystal jerked back from Kade and stared at Brent and Evan. What must they think, to see her standing here in Kade's arms, with him totally naked? To make matters worse, she realized that the warm water pouring over her had made the fabric of her dress essentially transparent. Her nipples were totally visible. And Kade's cock had begun to stiffen.

It was clear to Brent from the stricken look in Crystal's wide blue eyes that she thought he was angry to find her in Kade's arms; but he wasn't, and he was sure Evan wasn't, either. They both knew how much she loved them. As much as she might enjoy sex with Kade and that huge cock of his, Brent knew her heart belonged to him—and Evan. He also understood that she'd just been looking for a friend to talk to. He held back a grin. Only Crystal would find that friend in the form of a naked stud with a cock like a stallion's.

Brent stepped toward her, and Evan followed.

Kade turned toward them. "Hey, guys, there's nothing going on here."

Brent smiled. "I know." He walked toward Crystal, trying to ignore how her hard nipples showed clearly through the wet, transparent material of her dress.

Crystal sighed in relief at Brent's words.

"Kade, do you think we could have a moment alone with Crystal?" Brent asked.

"Yeah, of course." Kade reached past her and turned off the shower, then grabbed his towel from a nearby chair and walked across the lawn toward the villa.

She drew in a deep breath, trying to calm her uneven breathing as Brent and Evan stepped closer.

Brent took her hand. "Sweetheart, we need to talk."

She nodded. "I know. I heard Evan say he was going to take a job in New York, and . . ." She glanced from Brent to Evan, and her tears began to flow again. "Oh, Evan, I don't want you to go. There's got to be some way we can make this work out."

He smiled warmly and took her in his arms, ignoring the fact that her wet dress was soaking his shirt and shorts. He stroked her wet hair back from her face. "It's okay, gorgeous. Brent and I had a long talk, and"—he drew back and gazed into her eyes, his green eyes glowing with warmth—"we have a possible solution."

Hope surged within her. "What is it?"

Evan slid his arm around her waist and turned toward Brent.

Brent stepped closer and stroked her shoulder. "Well, you keep saying you don't want to choose between us."

She nodded.

"So Brent suggested that maybe we could work out something where you don't have to choose," Evan said.

"It would be a very unconventional arrangement, but we hope you like the idea."

She nodded again, ready to explode if they didn't tell her soon.

"We want to propose that all three of us stay together, in a committed relationship." Brent stroked her shoulder. "For a while, anyway, to see if it will work."

Her brows furrowed. "So we're just going to put off when I have to choose?"

"No, Brent just means that we need to take some time to figure out if we can make it work. There are a lot of things to figure out."

"And you'd be okay with this?" she asked Evan.

"Well, I already know that if you have to choose, you'll choose Brent," Evan said.

She gazed up at him and stroked his cheek. "Oh, Evan, I—"

He stopped her words with a kiss, then smiled down at her. "Don't apologize. I understand. But that gives me all the more reason to try and make this work. And sharing you with Brent is not only better than not having you at all"—he smiled warmly, then gazed at Brent with affection—"if we can make this work, it will be even better than anything I could have hoped for when I first told you how I felt about you." He locked gazes with her again and stroked her cheek. "Because what we can have with all three of us is so much more than I ever would have dreamed."

She could see love in his eyes—as he gazed at her now and when he was looking at Brent a moment ago.

"Brent and I have a whole new relationship," Evan continued, "making our friendship even deeper, and that's all because of you."

Evan took her hand in his, and Brent took her other hand.

"We have something very special together," Brent said. "We work as a team. The three of us—loving together, living together—will be sensational. The love and support we'll share will give us strength and happiness. We'll be an unbeatable team in life. "

"What about marriage and children?" she asked.

"Those are exactly the kinds of things we have to work out," Evan said. "But if we're all open to new ways of doing things—and this vacation has certainly shown we're willing to consider some pretty wild things—then we should be able to come up with something that will work for us."

"Crystal, are you okay not having a wedding? Or is it important to you to get married?" Brent asked.

"Because if it is," Evan said, "I can adapt to being the extra in the relationship if that's what you need."

Brent put his arm around Evan's shoulders. "I convinced him that even if he's not part of our marriage, if that's the way we go, that he'll never be on the outside looking in."

"What do you think?" Evan asked.

Both of them watched her uncertainly, awaiting her response. She drew in a deep breath. This was a big decision. It would be difficult, and different. Others wouldn't understand.

She smiled. But she didn't care about any of that. All

she cared about was that they would all be together. Committed to one another.

Warmth glowed inside her, and she squeezed their hands. "With all the love between us, I don't think any of us will ever feel like we're on the outside." A quivering smile claimed her face as joy catapulted through her. "So, yes. I love it. Absolutely, yes!"

She threw her arms around Brent and hugged him tightly, then kissed him passionately. Then she turned in his embrace, drawing his hands to her waist, and opened her arms to Evan. He stepped into her hug and kissed her.

When he finally released her, he stared at Crystal's breasts showing clearly through her soaking wet, white dress. She could see a growing bulge in his shorts.

"God, looking at you like that, woman, makes me want to tear that freaking dress off you and take you right here."

"Well, you know, Evan, we did catch her in another man's arms. I don't know about you, but I think that means some *punishment* is in order."

"Punishment?" she asked, her heart rate accelerating.

"Well, you must admit, you've been a very bad girl," Brent said.

Evan crossed his arms. "Kade was part of this. I think he needs to be punished, too."

Brent chuckled. "You're absolutely right."

Evan walked to the villa and went inside. A few moments later, he returned with a roll of gray tape in his hand and a broom handle. Kade, still naked, walked alongside him.

"Over to the bench," Evan instructed Kade.

Kade winked at Crystal, then walked to the elegant wooden-and-wrought-iron bench on the side of the patio. Evan gestured for him to sit down, then Evan wrapped some of the duct tape around Kade's wrist, then stretched his arm along the top of the bench and fastened his wrist to the wood. Evan fastened Kade's other wrist in the same way. He then wrapped tape around Kade's ankle, then drew a long strip around the leg of the bench, then back around his ankle again. Once both ankles were secured, Evan approached Crystal.

He stood in front of her and raised an eyebrow. "Hold out your arm."

She hesitated, then raised her arm. Evan wrapped tape around her upper arm, just above her elbow, then turned her around and pulled the tape behind her and wrapped it around her other arm, effectively locking her arms to her sides. He wrapped tape around her wrists in the same manner, pinning them by her hips and thighs. He turned her back to face him. Brent handed Evan the broom handle.

"This might be handy," Brent said.

Evan took it with a smile on his face. "You bet."

He crouched down, and Crystal felt him wrap tape around her ankle, then fasten it to the long wooden rod.

"Stand with your feet apart," Evan commanded.

She widened her stance.

"More."

After she obeyed, Evan attached her second ankle to the wooden rod.

She now stood with her legs wide apart and her arms

fixed at her sides. She felt open and vulnerable like this. She couldn't stop them from touching her intimate opening, from pushing into her. The thought sent thrills through her.

Evan stood and handed the tape to Brent, then grasped her skirt and lifted it, exposing her naked sex. He held the fabric bunched together like a cloth ponytail cascading off the side of her hip. Brent wrapped tape around the bundle, holding it like that—leaving her totally naked from the waist down.

"Hmm. I like that." Brent grinned, his hot gaze gliding over her clean-shaven folds.

Evan smiled as his hands stroked along her neck, then around behind, and he unfastened the tie on her halter-style dress. The fabric of her bodice fell forward, baring her wet breasts, and Brent tucked the loose fabric into the skirt so it didn't cover anything below her waist. Both men's gazes fell on her hard, puckered nipples.

"It looks like you were really turned on seeing Kade naked." Brent's hand glided over her nipple lightly, sending need rocketing though her, then slipped away.

"Were you?" Evan demanded.

She nodded, wide-eyed.

He leaned in close to her ear. "I can't hear you. When I ask you a question, I want you to answer me. Do you understand?"

A quiver rushed through her at his no-nonsense tone. She had seen Evan like this only once before, briefly with Sarah, and she had to admit it turned her on.

"Yes, sir."

"Yes, sir, what?"

"Yes, sir. I was very turned on seeing Kade naked."

"Why?"

Okay, that's how he wanted to play this.

"Because his cock is so big, sir." Her insides clenched at the thought.

He nudged his head toward Kade sitting on the bench behind him. "So you like his big cock?"

Crystal glanced toward Kade, naked and bound to the bench, his semi-erect cock amazingly long and thick.

She licked her lips. "Yes, I like his big cock."

"I can tell you'd like to take it in your mouth right now. You want to suck on it. Is that right?"

She licked her lips as she imagined his hard flesh filling her mouth. "Yes, sir. I want to suck on Kade's big cock."

"But you're being punished, so that's not going to happen."

"That's right," Brent agreed. He walked toward Kade, then crouched in front of him. "But I think you should see what you're missing."

Crystal's heartbeat stuttered as Brent wrapped his big, masculine hand around Kade's cock and stroked it. Kade's cock quickly grew fully erect. Brent leaned forward and wrapped his lips around the tip. Crystal's breath caught as the huge cockhead disappeared into Brent's mouth.

"Hey, I didn't know I was missing out on a party." Sarah closed the sliding door behind her and sauntered across the patio, wearing a pink terry robe. "If I'd known, I would have skipped shopping."

"This isn't a party," Evan said in a stern voice, but he

winked at her. "We caught Kade and Crystal together and we've decided they both need to be punished."

"Oh, I see." Sarah unfastened the tie at her waist and opened her robe, exposing her totally naked body. The robe dropped to the ground. "Well, I should be punished, too. After all, I encouraged this kind of behavior."

"I see. You're right. You should be punished, too." Evan walked toward Kade and Brent. "Crystal admitted that she wants to suck Kade's big cock. Of course, we won't allow her to do that, so we're showing her what she's missing."

"I could help with that," Sarah offered.

"Right now, I want you to sit beside him on the bench."

Sarah walked toward the bench, her beautiful naked body swaying sexily, then sat on the far side of the bench and watched Brent. Brent released Kade's cock from his mouth and shifted to one side as Evan crouched on the other side. Evan leaned forward and ran his lips along the side of Kade's generous cock. Brent mirrored his actions on the other side of the huge shaft. Crystal watched her men stroke their lips and tongues along Kade's huge erection, heat building within her. The men moved up and down, then nuzzled the base. When they glided up this time, they continued off the end and their lips met. Her insides melted as her two men's mouths moved on each other.

# Twenty-five

Evan opened his mouth as Brent's tongue slid inside. His friend's hot, hard mouth against his set a fire within him. God, this was erotic and bad-assed, not caring what anyone thought, just doing what felt good. Especially knowing there were two sexy women watching and getting mega turned on.

He drew away from Brent and turned to Kade. He licked Kade's bead-hard nipple while his hand wrapped around the guy's monstrous cock. He felt Brent's mouth brush his hand as Brent took Kade's cock in his mouth again.

Evan stood up and stripped off his clothes, watching Brent's mouth moving on Kade's big shaft. Evan then wrapped his hand around his own aching cock, longing for a hot mouth around it, and moved in front of Kade. He pressed his cockhead to Kade's mouth, and Kade opened. Evan fed his long shaft into Kade's mouth. Kade took him deep, then began sucking.

Brent stood and peeled away his clothes, then walked to Sarah. She grabbed his stiff cock and took it into her mouth. Evan watched her red lips surround Brent's erection as Kade sucked Evan's cock. While she continued to devour Brent's cock, Sarah's hand stroked Evan's hip, then over his ass. Her fingers danced over Evan's balls from behind, then glided away and found his back opening. Evan stiffened a little when he felt a finger push into his ass but gradually relaxed as Sarah stroked inside.

Kade swirled his tongue around Evan's cockhead as Sarah's finger continued to stroke. Intense pleasure built within Evan, and he sucked in air. Kade sucked hard while Sarah's talented finger continued stroking Evan's anus. Heat shuddered through him and he knew he would soon blow. Sarah's thumb pressed on Evan's perineum and pleasure exploded through him. Intense and mind-blowing. Evan groaned as he ejaculated into Kade's mouth.

Crystal watched as Kade and Sarah brought Evan to climax. Beside them, Brent's cock glided in and out of Sarah's mouth like a piston. Suddenly he drove forward and shuddered, clearly filling Sarah with his semen.

This was true punishment, since she ached so badly for her own release. She desperately wanted someone to come over and touch her, to lick her—to fuck her.

"Stand up." Brent held out his hand to Sarah and helped her to her feet. He sat down and drew her in front of him, then leaned forward and licked her intimate folds.

Evan crouched behind her and guided her to open

her legs, then began licking her from behind. Occasionally, their tongues would connect and they'd stop to twine them together between her thighs and kiss. Then they'd lick her again. Yearning filled Crystal at the need burning through her. Sarah threw back her head, her long blonde hair falling in glistening waves across her back. Beside them, Kade's cock towered in the air.

Evan grasped Sarah's hips, then guided her away from Brent and positioned her in front of Kade.

"Bend over and suck his cock," Evan instructed.

Sarah bent at the waist, exposing an eyeful of blonde curls. As she dove down on Kade, Crystal noticed that Evan was gliding a condom over his cock, then he pressed his cockhead to Sarah's exposed opening and pushed forward. Crystal almost cried out at the erotic sight of his hard erection disappearing into Sarah's slick flesh. Brent wrapped his hand around his own cock and moved to stand beside Kade. He pressed his cockhead to Kade's lips, and Kade opened and took him inside his mouth.

Heat simmered through Crystal, and her groin ached with need. Evan began pumping into Sarah, and Brent pushed his cock deeper into Kade's mouth.

After a few erotically charged moments, Sarah tugged Kade's cock from her mouth and groaned.

"Oh, God, I'm going to come." She sucked in air, then moaned as Evan continued to fill her with his long, hard shaft.

Her moan turned to a feral cry as she plunged into orgasm. Her hand stroked up and down Kade's long shaft. Brent groaned, and immediately after that Evan joined him.

Sarah licked Kade's cockhead, then glided down on him, but Evan coiled his hand in her hair and drew her head back.

"No, I don't want him to come yet." Evan released Sarah's hair and helped her to her feet. "Now go over to Crystal and . . ." He leaned toward her ear and murmured something Crystal couldn't hear but had little doubt as to the intent.

Sarah strolled toward Crystal with a sly smile. She cupped Crystal's face between her hands and joined lips with her. The softness of Sarah's tongue as it prodded her lips, then slid into her mouth, excited Crystal. Sarah's kiss was so different from a man's hard-lipped, consuming style. Crystal opened to her. Heat flooded through her and she longed for more.

Sarah glided downward, kissing along Crystal's neck, then down her chest. Her lips found one of Crystal's hard nipples, and Crystal gasped. Sarah licked her nub, then sucked lightly. When Sarah's mouth abandoned her, Crystal shook her head. Then Sarah licked her other nipple and sucked it deep into her mouth.

"Oh, yes." Crystal's head lolled from side to side, the tile wall hard behind her.

"Do you want more?" Evan asked.

"Yes. Please, yes."

Sarah rested her hand on Crystal's belly, then glided downward. When her finger glided over Crystal's slick opening, then dipped inside, Crystal moaned.

"She's very wet," Sarah said.

"Good. Now come here, Sarah."

"No," Crystal wailed as Sarah drew her finger free and walked away.

"What is it you want, Crystal?" Brent asked.

"You know what I want," she whimpered.

He grinned. "That's true, but tell us anyway."

"I want to be fucked."

"By whom?" Evan asked.

She glanced at Kade's big cock. Hard and long. God, she wanted it inside her, but saying so would probably lead to more punishment.

"By you. And Brent."

Brent chuckled. "What about Kade?"

Delicious frustration quivered through her. What answer would get her fucked sooner?

"Only if it pleases the two of you," she responded.

Evan laughed. "Liar." He glanced toward Kade's gigantic cock, still standing at full attention. "I'm sure you want that huge cock driving into you right now." He glanced at her again. "Don't deny it."

She said nothing. Right now, she just wanted a cock inside her.

"Just admit it," Brent said, "and we'll let you have what you want."

"You will?" she asked uncertainly. Her gaze drifted to Kade's tower of hard flesh, and her insides clenched. God, it would feel sensational pushing into her.

"Of course," Brent responded. "Just tell us you want Kade's cock inside you."

She nodded. "I do. I want Kade's cock inside me." She was careful to use the same phrasing as Brent, knowing that doing otherwise could be grounds for more punishment—like denying her that big cock.

"Good." Brent walked toward her and took hold of her bound arm and guided her forward.

It was tough walking with her ankles attached to the wooden broom handle, forcing her legs wide. She hobbled along beside Brent. Once they reached the bench, rather than stopping in front of Kade, he led her behind it.

"You'll get your wish in a minute." He grabbed a beach towel that lay on a chair by the patio table, then returned to the bench and draped the folded towel over the back beside Kade. In fact, over Kade's outstretched arm.

"Lean forward."

Brent guided her forward until her ribs rested on the towel and the undersides of her naked breasts rested against Kade's muscular arm. Her ass stuck up in the air, and with her ankles attached to the wooden rod, forcing her legs wide, she knew her damp opening was fully exposed.

She felt a warm tongue push against her and drag along her wet flesh. She moaned at the exquisite sensation. Evan and Sarah moved behind her. A second mouth replaced the first, and a tongue toyed with her clit. Another mouth pressed to her opening, a tongue flicking inside her. Her eyelids fell closed as the mouths shifted and moved, teasing her. Flicking her clit and sending her pleasure soaring. Bringing her close to orgasm, then backing off.

Then they slipped away. She felt hands on her upper arms and she was drawn to a standing position again. She glanced over her shoulder to see that Brent was the one touching her. He walked her back to the front of the bench, then turned her so her back faced Kade, then he backed her up.

"Sit."

She gazed questioningly at Brent, but he simply took her arms, steadying her as he eased her downward. Before she was all the way down, he grasped Kade's cock, now encased in a condom, and pressed it to her slick opening, then continued to lower her onto Kade's lap. She sucked in air as the enormous shaft of hot flesh pushed into her, stretching her opening as it glided inside. When she finally sat squarely on Kade's lap, his cock filled her so full that she thought she'd burst.

Evan took Sarah's hand and led her to the table, then he leaned against it. He pulled her into his arms and kissed her. Brent stepped behind her and stroked her round ass. One of his hands glided between her legs and stroked over her slick folds.

Crystal tightened around Kade, wanting him to move within her. To fuck her. But she realized with his arms and legs fastened snugly to the bench, he couldn't do much more than just sit there. Similarly, with her arms bound and her legs immobilized, she couldn't get enough balance to move up and down on him. God, a big old cock inside her, just as she'd wanted, but she couldn't do anything but squeeze it. And watch Brent and Evan roll condoms over their stiff shafts.

Evan grabbed his cock and pressed it to Sarah's opening while Brent stroked her breasts from behind, his big hands covering her. Crystal wished Kade's hands were free so he could fondle her aching breasts.

Sarah was fully impaled by Evan. Brent stroked her ass, then drew her buttocks wide. He pressed his cockhead to her opening, then slowly glided inside.

"That's right, honey. Push it inside." Sarah's face glowed with delight as Brent pushed deeper into her.

Once he was fully immersed, the three stilled, Sarah sandwiched between the two hard, male bodies. Then they began to move. The two cocks drawing back, then driving into her again in unison. The speed of their thrusts increased and Sarah's eyes fell closed.

"Oh, yeah. Fuck me." She gasped. "Yes, I'm so close."

Their bodies slapped together. The sound of flesh hitting flesh filled the yard. Crystal shifted a little and squeezed Kade's hard cock, but it didn't do enough. He groaned as she squeezed again. His lips grazed the back of her neck, sending shivers down her spine.

"Oh, God, I want you to fuck me." She dropped her head against his chest and neck, and he nuzzled her ear.

"Believe me, I want to fuck you just as much," he murmured.

Sarah moaned as the two men fucked her hard. She gasped, then wailed in release. Brent's face contorted, then he groaned, followed in quick succession by Evan. Finally, the three of them collapsed together.

A small whimper escaped Crystal. Brent, Sarah, and Evan separated, then the men pulled off the condoms, placed them on the side of the patio, and walked toward her. One look at their wilted cocks and she knew neither of them would fuck her soon.

"Please let Kade fuck me."

"I don't think that's a good idea," Evan said. "Do you, Brent?"

"Well, she does seem desperate. Maybe we should let her."

"But allowing another man to fuck her . . . ?" Evan shook his head. "We can't really allow that. After all, that's why we're punishing her."

Brent scratched his head. "Well, I have an idea."

# Twenty-six

Crystal stared at them imploringly. "Please, I'll do anything."

Brent chuckled. "Good, because Evan and I will need a little help from you."

Then he grabbed Evan's arm and led him toward the pool. Crystal groaned at their retreat. When they were too far away for her to hear, Brent murmured to Evan. Evan's eyes widened, but then he nodded. Then the two of them dove into the pool. Seconds later, they stepped out of the water and walked toward her, their big, muscular bodies dripping wet and glistening in the sunshine.

Evan moved close to her, his hand wrapped around his wilted cock. He pressed it to her lips and she opened. His cool, wet cock slid into her mouth. She squeezed around his soft flesh and sucked the water from him. Immediately, he began to harden. She twirled her tongue around his tip. He pushed deeper and she opened her throat. Oh,

God, she loved having his swelling cock in her mouth. He filled her, then drew back. He slid from her mouth and wrapped his hand around his now warm and hard cock.

Brent stepped forward and glided his semi-erect cock into her mouth. She licked and sucked him, thrilling at the feel of his hardness inside her. When he moved away, Evan took her shoulders and drew her to her feet. Need quivered through her as Kade's hard cock caressed her inner passage, then fell away.

As Brent and Evan guided her toward the shower again, Sarah produced scissors and snipped the tape fastening Kade to the bench. Evan positioned Crystal against the shower wall, her back pressed against the cold tiles. Kade and Sarah joined them.

"Do you want to fuck Crystal?" Brent asked Kade.

"Oh, yeah."

"And, like Crystal, will you do anything for that goal?"

Kade grinned. "Absolutely."

"Good. You're going to be our fuck puppet. But we won't be using our hands to guide you like with a normal puppet." Brent took a bottle from Sarah and two condom packets and handed them to Kade. "You know what to do with these?"

Kade took the items. "I have a pretty good idea."

He tore open one of the small packets, then pressed the condom to the tip of Brent's erection and rolled it into place. He opened the bottle and squeezed clear gel onto his hand, then wrapped his other hand around Brent's hard cock and applied the gel in spiral strokes. Once he was finished, Brent's cock glistened with the film of lubricant.

Evan stepped forward and Kade repeated the process. Crystal licked her lips at the sight of Kade's big masculine hand stroking around and around Evan's hard cock.

When Kade finally finished, she gazed at Brent's and Evan's slick cocks, wishing any one of the men would drive inside her.

Brent couldn't believe how far they were going with this sexual escapade. But why the hell not? This was about sex and being free and wild. And as far as he was concerned, it didn't get any wilder than this.

"Now what did you say you wanted, Crystal?"

The hunger in her eyes turned him on more than anything. The tip of her tongue dragged along her lips, and she gazed at him uncertainly.

"I want to be fucked."

"No, that's not it. Tell me exactly what you said."

"I . . . uh . . . said please let Kade fuck me."

"Now tell Kade what you want. And assume he doesn't want to. Convince him."

She drew in a deep breath. "Kade, I want you so bad. Please fuck me." Her gaze dropped to his huge condom-covered shaft, and she licked her lips. "Please drive that huge cock of yours deep into me."

At her heartfelt words, Brent could barely stop himself from lurching forward and driving into her. But he held himself back.

"Kade, you heard her," Evan said. "Go and shove your enormous dick into her."

Kade grinned and stepped toward her. He cupped her cheeks and kissed her, his lips lingering for a second, then he wrapped his hand around his big cock and pressed it to her wet opening. But he didn't thrust in right away. He dragged his cockhead over her slick folds, teasing her. Then he settled his mushroom tip against her and eased forward. From the look of rapture on her face, the pleasure of his invasion was excruciating, and that sent Brent's hormones rocketing into overdrive.

"Oh, God, yes. That feels so good."

Once Kade was fully immersed in her, Brent stepped up behind Kade. He cupped Kade's hard butt and separated, just as he had with Sarah, then he pressed his cockhead to the puckered opening. God, he'd never done this with a man, but what was a real turn-on was that Kade's cock was deep inside Crystal right now. She was probably squeezing him inside her to get more stimulation. At that thought, Brent eased forward. Kade's tight passage squeezed him as he moved steadily forward. Finally, Brent's entire cock was inside. He grasped Kade's hips.

"Now, Crystal, I'm going to fuck you with Kade's big cock. Are you ready?"

"Oh, God, yes."

"How about you, Kade?" Brent asked.

"Yeah, man. Go for it."

Crystal thrilled at the feel of Kade's big cock inside her and was doubly turned on knowing Brent was inside Kade. Kade's cock moved away, then drove deep into her. Then it drew away and filled her again. Driven by Brent. Both men fucking her.

Escalating need swamped her senses as the big cock filled her again and again, driving her against the tiled wall. The thick cock stretched her, stroking her insides. Wild, erotic sensations danced along her nerve endings, and intense pleasure uncoiled inside her like a flower.

Kade's big cock filled her, but Brent was fucking her. The thought sent her spiraling toward ecstasy.

"Oh, it feels so—" She gasped in pleasure. "I'm so . . . ah!" Joyful sensations careened through her, then she flew into a state of absolute bliss.

Brent groaned at the feel of Kade's tight passage squeezing his aching cock as they drove into Crystal's pussy. At Crystal's moan, Brent erupted in orgasm, pleasure tearing from him in an intense climax.

As he relaxed, he realized Kade had not released yet, but that was good. Because they weren't finished.

Brent drew back, pulling his cock from Kade's ass. As he stepped back, peeling away the condom, Evan positioned himself behind Kade and pushed his cock into him. The sight of Evan's cock disappearing into Kade sent a thrill through Brent.

Evan began to move, fucking Crystal through Kade. Crystal moaned and tossed her head back and forth. She plummeted into orgasm again, her cries acting like an aphrodisiac. Evan groaned his release, then Kade also groaned, his face contorted in ecstasy.

"God, you three are so fucking sexy to watch," Brent said.

As soon as they moved away, Brent knew he had to feel Crystal around him. Directly. He needed to be inside her.

He moved to her, then took her in his arms and kissed her. He pushed his cock against her and glided inside her slick opening. The feel of her hot, wet opening surrounding him was paradise.

"Brent, wait a second," Sarah said. "I have an idea. I bet both you and Evan want to be inside Crystal right now. And given that Crystal has been stretched by Kade's huge tool, I think that's entirely possible. But you have to give me a second to get Evan ready."

Brent was deep inside Crystal, and her heavy breaths pushed her breasts hard against him, playing havoc with his hormones. And his patience. He glanced over his shoulder to see Sarah drag the condom from Evan's soft cock, then crouch in front of him and lick his shaft, then suck it into her mouth.

A few short moments later, Evan stood at full attention. He stepped beside Brent, and Sarah guided his cock to Crystal's wet pussy. Brent drew out a little and allowed Sarah to press Evan's hard flesh tight to his, then she guided them into Crystal's opening. Brent was amazed when both cockheads slid into her.

Crystal's tiny whimper of pleasure set Brent's cock throbbing.

"Oh, God, that feels incredible." The sweet sound of Crystal's breathless voice coiled through him.

Brent wrapped his arm around Evan's waist so they could move in unison. Evan reciprocated.

Crystal couldn't believe both their cocks were inside her. Both in her slick, needy vagina. She also couldn't believe she still needed them so badly. But that must be what love did to a gal.

They drove in deep and she gasped. Their cocks stroked her insides and she sagged against the wall, enjoying the feel of them filling her again and again. Two big, hard cocks. Two men who loved her driving her to ecstatic heights.

They pushed deep and hard, pinning her to the wall, and they both groaned. The feel of the two cocks gushing into her sent her over the edge. She wailed, spiraling off to ecstasy yet again.

The soft ocean breeze brushed Crystal's cheek, swirling strands of hair in her face. She brushed it back as she walked along the beach toward the villa, Brent and Evan by her side. Brent opened the back gate and they walked up the steps and crossed the yard together.

What they'd just done was exciting, but even more exciting was the fact that she had an amazing new relationship to look forward to, with both Brent *and* Evan.

Once they were in the sunroom and Evan closed the door behind them, Crystal turned to face them with a big smile. "I'm so glad you two worked everything out."

Evan stepped toward her and cupped her face. As he

leaned in close, she lost herself in the love glowing from his eyes.

"Believe me, so am I."

When Evan's lips met hers, she melted against him, her arms curling around his shoulders. Brent's arms slid around her from behind and she felt totally surrounded in love.

Oh, God, they both wanted her. And they wanted each other. Together the three of them would start a life together. Living and loving together.

When she'd awakened on her wedding day, knowing she would soon walk down the aisle with the man she loved and looking forward to her dream-come-true honeymoon, she'd never dreamed it would end this way. She smiled, knowing she would never lose this insatiable desire for her two very special men.

Who would have thought that being abandoned at the altar on her wedding day would be the best thing that ever happened to her?

*Don't miss*
*Opal Carew's next novel*

# Illicit

*Coming July 2012 from St. Martin's Griffin*

# Fulfill all your wildest fantasies with Opal Carew...

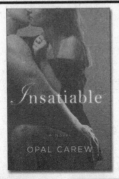

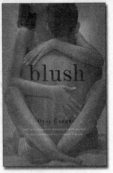